The BFF Bucket List

by DEE ROMITO

ALADDIN

New York   London   Toronto   Sydney   New Delhi

For my mom—
my BFF from the moment we met
♥

ALADDIN
An imprint of Simon & Schuster Children's Publishing Division
1230 Avenue of the Americas, New York, New York 10020
First Aladdin hardcover edition May 2016
Text copyright © 2016 by Simon & Schuster, Inc.
Jacket illustration copyright © 2016 by Annabelle Metayer
Also available in an Aladdin M!X edition.
All rights reserved, including the right of reproduction
in whole or in part in any form.
ALADDIN is a trademark of Simon & Schuster, Inc., and related logo
is a registered trademark of Simon & Schuster, Inc.
For information about special discounts for bulk purchases,
please contact Simon & Schuster Special Sales at 1-866-506-1949
or business@simonandschuster.com.
The Simon & Schuster Speakers Bureau can bring authors to your
live event. For more information or to book an event contact
the Simon & Schuster Speakers Bureau at 1-866-248-3049
or visit our website at www.simonspeakers.com.
Book designed by Karina Granda
The text of this book was set in Bembo STD.
Manufactured in the United States of America 0416 FFG
2 4 6 8 10 9 7 5 3 1
Library of Congress Control Number 2015959870
ISBN 978-1-4814-4643-3 (hc)
ISBN 978-1-4814-4642-6 (pbk)
ISBN 978-1-4814-4644-0 (eBook)

CHAPTER ONE

Ella

PISTACHIO ICE CREAM.

It's all that stands between two best friends and flavor number forty-seven on the big board at Three Scoops. We've worked our entire eighth grade year for this. One more to go, and then summer can officially begin with our mission accomplished.

> **Rule #1:** You *cannot* choose a flavor that's been crossed off the list.

> **Rule #2:** You must share with your BFF. (Kill two flavors with one spoon!)

Rule #3: Totally gross = bring home to unsuspecting little brother

Skyler sits across the booth from me, plastic spoon in hand. "You go first, Ella," she says.

Sure, easy for her to say. She had praline crunch.

"I can't do it." I shift in my chair, scooting away from the green glop in my bowl. "There's a reason we picked forty-six other flavors before this one. Well, technically forty-five for me." It drove me crazy to have to skip a flavor, but key lime pie wouldn't have been worth the allergic reaction.

"That was a medical pass. But you're not getting out of this one," says Skyler.

I wait for us to go back and forth, me giving reasons why I shouldn't and hearing why I absolutely have to eat it. I wait for her face to scrunch up, and for her to comment about how awful this is. Instead, Skyler reaches across the table and jabs her spoon into the ice cream.

"Let's get this over with," she says, shoving a bigger-than-required spoonful into her mouth. She swallows quickly and motions toward me. "Your turn."

Wait, what? We're supposed to find a million reasons to drag this out until we're one minute away from missing our curfew.

Skyler's phone beeps, and she looks down at the screen.

"What's going on?" I ask.

"Well, we might need to leave early," says Skyler.

"Early? Why? Do we have other plans?" I ask, squeezing all three questions into about one point five seconds.

Skyler leans forward on the table and motions for me to do the same. We're almost forehead to forehead in prime whisper position.

"What do you think about doing something different tonight?" she asks. "You know, not our usual hanging out at one of our houses."

It's like we're in spy mode. "Like what?" I whisper as if she's going to suggest an international covert operation.

"Like a scary movie," says Skyler.

I jolt back and sit upright. "We don't like scary movies."

Skyler leans her head against the soft cushion of the booth. "*You* don't like scary movies, Ella. So I never suggest them. But I'd like to try something new for a change."

"Oh," I say, my shoulders slumping.

"Brooke's mom said she could have some friends over for a movie night, and we're invited," says Skyler.

I wait to see if she's finished because I'm pretty sure she's not. "And I want to go."

Brooke seems nice enough, although I don't know her very well since we've only been in one class together. But scary movies, with the possibility of spiders and blood and people jumping out from behind trees? No. Thank. You.

"And I don't want to go," I say.

Just like that, instead of undercover spies on a secret mission, we're Wild West cowboys in a tense standoff. There's a baby crying, a couple snuggled into a booth in the corner, and a group of older teenagers laughing hysterically. And then there's me and Skyler, sitting silently.

"Maybe I should just go and we can meet up tomorrow?" says Skyler. She turns on her puppy-dog eyes, silently begging me to let her off the hook. But I know she'll stay if I ask her to.

"We were supposed to celebrate," I say. "We can finally order our favorite flavors again."

Her eyes are pleading, and oh my pistachio, I really don't want to be a jerk about this. It's my best friend duty to give her a pass, right?

"Have fun," I finally say. "I'll see you tomorrow, right?"

"Of course," says Skyler. "Like I could ever go more than a day without you."

We laugh that one-ha kind of laugh where you don't even need the rest.

"You're the best, Ella." Skyler hops out of the booth and leans down to give me a hug. She's out the door and back on her phone in no time at all.

I poke my spoon at the pistachio ice cream and prepare to finish the mission solo. My taste buds fight me every step of the way, but I manage to swallow it anyway. Let's just say I would have preferred one called Alligator Chunk Surprise.

I text my mom to come pick me up early. And, because why not, I take another bite.

I'm used to waiting for Skyler because she's always twelve minutes late. Always. I don't think she means to be, but I notice these things. Twelve minutes. Exactly.

"Honey, Skyler's here," Mom yells up the stairs. A few second later, there's a quick *thump, thump, thump* of footsteps on the wooden stairs. I scoot over on the bed to make room for what I know is coming. Skyler belly flops on the mattress, face-planting into the lacy throw pillow. For someone who is so proud of being a free spirit, she's insanely predictable.

Skyler flips over and stares up at the ceiling. "I met a *really* cute boy, Ella."

Here we go again. Whenever Skyler mentions a "really cute boy," I know she's already head over heels.

"Okay, okay, but give me a minute." I walk over to my bookshelf and pick up one of the memory boxes we've been keeping since kindergarten. It's full of photos and trinkets—we'll definitely need a new one for high school.

I sit down at my desk ready to add to the collection. "What do you have for me?"

She pulls a penny out of her pocket.

I reach over and grab it, inspecting the shiny copper coating in the sunlight that's gleaming through the window. "Should I even ask what this has to do with the mystery boy?"

Skyler sits up and sighs. "We all went to The Donut last night after the movie. He was in line."

The Donut is the neighborhood hangout when we're not at Three Scoops. The building is actually shaped like a doughnut that's lying flat and people always give directions based on our town's famous landmark.

"Head north and turn left at The Donut."

"Keep going until you see The Donut. Can't miss it."

No, seriously, you can't.

"He didn't even realize he dropped the penny,"

Skyler continues, "and I had to act like I was adjusting my flip-flop in order to get it without looking like a complete tool."

"So does 'the one' have a name?" I ask as I glue-stick the back of the penny and start a new page.

"I have no idea," says Skyler. "But I overheard him talking about Jefferson High and freshman year. Maybe he went to Adams Middle?"

Two middle schools filter into Jefferson High. Ours is Washington Middle, and Adams is on the other side of town. Next year will be full of new faces.

Skyler can't wait.

I can't eat enough Starbursts—my favorite candy—to calm myself down whenever I think about it.

Without waiting for an answer, Skyler changes the subject. "So, Brooke's going to the bowling alley later. She says some kids from Adams will be there too. We should totally go."

Bowling with Skyler would be great—I can never get her to go—but it won't be just me and Skyler. "Will we know anyone?" I ask.

"You know Brooke," Skyler points out. "And I'm sure kids from school will show up."

I add a pleading to my voice. "Can't we stay here and hang out? I'd rather it was just us."

Skyler crosses her legs at the ankles and fiddles with one of her chunky rings. "It's summer, Ella. We can hang out here anytime, but everyone's going out *tonight*."

My mind is spinning with how to respond, and I'm way too aware of my breathing. Why is this so incredibly awkward right now?

"Come with me?" asks Skyler, getting up. She's made her decision.

I turn from side to side in my wheelie desk chair. "I think I'm gonna stay home."

We sit without talking for what is most certainly forever, but when I check the clock, only a minute has passed.

"I'll try not to stay late so I can text you when I get home, okay?" says Skyler.

"Sure." I swing my chair back to the desk and smooth the penny down onto the paper. "Let me know if Penny Boy is there."

Skyler tousles my brown curls on the way out the door, and the smell of today's conditioner choice floats through the air. "Ooh, peach," she says. "Who needs a calendar when I have your hair-care routine to tell me what day it is?"

She laughs and we wave like we always do—as if we're princesses—but for some reason it feels like a bigger good-bye than usual.

CHAPTER TWO

Skyler

I'VE NEVER FELT WEIRD LEAVING ELLA'S house. Like, ever. I hate this feeling.

What doesn't sound fun about hanging out at a bowling alley with a bunch of friends? I mean, yeah, I don't bowl, but the hanging out part and the friends part? I'm all over that.

It's crowded when I get here, so I scan the sea of people for someone I know. And there's Travis, my next door neighbor who's supersweet but also slightly annoying. I mean the boy is 200 percent Gorgeous with a capital G, but he has no filter when it comes to social skills and uses the phrase "cray cray" like he earns a dollar every time he says it. And once he has your attention, he won't stop talking. He cornered me yesterday when I went to get the mail. I said I had to go to the bathroom and never came back.

I try to duck behind a pillar, but my swiftness needs some major work. "Major Work," I say with a salute but then quickly realize Ella isn't here to appreciate the joke.

"Did you just salute me?" Travis pokes his head around the pillar. Without the bathroom excuse, I'm out of ideas in my getaway box. "That's cray cray."

"Nope, just brushing hair out of my face." I push another strand off my forehead as if that makes my case. "How's it going, Travis?"

He stares at me for way too long, and I can't tell if there's really something in that brain of his or if he's off in space somewhere. "That was a *long* trip to the bathroom yesterday," he says. "I waited for like an hour. Everything okay?"

This kid's tone is impossible to read. Is he actually concerned or is he making me own up to ditching him?

"Everything's good. Sorry, I had some things to do in the house." I don't elaborate. To my left, I catch a glimpse of Brooke and couldn't be more relieved. "Oh, there's my friend. I gotta go. Nice chatting with you." I sprint over to Brooke, grab her by the arm, and guide her out of Travis's field of view.

"What's that about?" she asks. "That boy is adorable. I wish he'd been in more of my classes in middle school. Maybe next year."

"Trust me, don't judge a book by its cover," I say.

Brooke shakes her head at me. "Where's Ella?"

"Oh, um, she couldn't come out tonight." Feeling guilty, I reach in my pocket for my phone to text Ella. "Hang on a sec," I say. But that's when he appears across the room. I grab Brooke by the shoulders and turn her in the other direction. "Oh my god, it's Penny Boy."

And he's smiling at me.

Ella! Penny Boy is HERE. What do I do?

I don't know how long I can wait for her reply. I'm crouched behind the end of the counter like a four-year-old playing hide-and-seek.

"Excuse me, Miss. Your shoes?" The cashier holds a pair of size six bowling shoes out for me.

I reach my hand up and grab them, throwing a five-dollar bill on the counter. "Thanks. Keep the change."

"Um, it's six-dollars and fifty cents for the shoes and the game," he says.

"Six fifty? For these shoes?" Brooke has insisted I join in, so I have no choice.

I pay up and scoot over to a table out of the way to put on the shoes. My phone beeps with a text from Ella.

> The Queen of Flirting is asking ME for advice? lol.
> Go say hi. Flip your hair or something.

> But I'm terrified to talk to him.

As I hit send, I'm sure she's wondering if it's really me. I've never been afraid to talk to anyone before.

> Maybe Brooke has an idea? Gotta go. Watching
> movie with little bro.

I wait for an lol or a smiley face, but they don't come.

Ella's right. I am the Queen of Flirting. I can totally do this. I stand up tall in my disgustingly red-and-tan mosaic shoes, convincing myself that the cute summer dress and my long, shiny locks will take the focus off the not-so-fashionable footwear. I take long strides to the lane where Brooke is waiting for me.

The place is packed. Bowling teams with embroidered jerseys line the alleyways and crowds of middle schoolers and high schoolers fill in the rest. I focus on Brooke and make it my goal simply to get to her. Penny Boy probably won't even notice me in all this chaos.

This isn't so hard, I think to myself.

But then it happens. In one huge whirlwind.

Penny Boy is in my sight.

He waves.

I attempt to wave back, but before I can lift my hand in the air . . . I slip on the freshly shined floor.

My legs come out from under me.

I land. With a thud.

On my butt.

"Oh my god, Skyler, are you okay?" Brooke is standing over me, holding out her hand.

Ouch. Ouch. Ouch!

I grab onto her with one hand and use the other to shield my face. "Please tell me Penny Boy did not see that. Seriously, lie to me if you have to."

She squeezes her lips together and doesn't say a word. A group of kids has gathered around me, and the sound of bowling balls dropping is now practically nonexistent.

"Okay, okay, go back to your games, people," says

Brooke's friend Quinn, her voice echoing through the place. "Nothing to see here." Her face is turned toward the crowd, not me, but I can see her messy, brown bob from behind as she ushers people away.

Quinn pulls me up and helps me to a colorful, plastic, very uncomfortable seat. The instant I sit, a bolt of pain shoots up from my tailbone.

Ouch. Ouch. Triple ouch!

I know without a doubt that while he is "Penny Boy" to me, I am most certainly "That girl who fell on her butt" to him.

Wait until Ella hears about this.

CHAPTER THREE

Ella

THE MOVIE MY LITTLE BROTHER, NICHOLAS,
picked out last night had me nodding off way before a
decent bedtime. He had to wake me up and poke me
up the stairs into bed when it was over. Yes, poke. He
takes his lightsaber duties a little too seriously.

"Cut it out, young Padawan," I remember saying in
a groggy voice.

"To the dungeon, Princess Leia." *Poke, poke, poke.*

I didn't mention that the dungeon wouldn't be
*up*stairs.

I wake up to the sound of a typewriter going off
from my cell phone. A text from Skyler.

Too late last night to message you, but OMG.
Wait until you hear this.

I'm sure she has a great story. Bowling was probably superamazingly fun last night. And I missed it. All the things Skyler is excited about form a list in my head. Because that's how I always think—in lists and rules.

1. Have an amazing summer

2. Hang out with friends

3. Meet cute boys

4. Go to high school

5. Take new classes but don't try too hard

6. Meet cute boys

They're all different from what I'd put on my list, except number one—have an amazing summer. And I wonder how that's possible when my BFF and I don't ever want to do the same things anymore. Mine goes something like this:

16

1. Have an amazing summer with Skyler

2. Watch (non-scary!) movies

3. Look at cute boys from across the room,
but never actually do anything about it

4. Avoid thinking about high school for as
long as possible

5. Panic about new classes and work my
butt off to make the honor roll

6. Get 100 percent embarrassed when a
boy talks to me. (IF a boy ever talks to me)

I sigh and remember I need to respond to Skyler's
text.

Want to come over and tell me about it?

She answers with a capital letter shout and a total of
four exclamation points.

YES!! Be there by ten!!

I take that all as a good sign. But still, the energy has drained from my body as I imagine all the ways she'll be moving on without me this summer and especially in high school.

Unless . . . I rewrite those lists.

I jump out of bed and head to my desk, pulling out a notebook and pen from the drawer.

Yes, yes, yes, *this* is the answer to saving our friendship from high-school-tear-apart disaster, which I refuse to let happen. What would I ever do without Skyler?

We'll have that amazing summer, doing all the things we've always wanted to. Plus crazy things. Things I'd never in a million years do without Skyler by my side. And I promise myself I'll include the "Seriously, Ella, we *have* to do this someday" things only Skyler would put on there. Because if it means holding on to our friendship, I'm so in.

I type "best friend summer bucket list" in the search box on my computer screen and get over thirteen million results. Thirteen *million*. The idea that other friends all over the world are doing the same thing makes me smile. I read through the first ten links and make mental notes of what I'm sure will be Skyler's favorites (skipping the no-way-José-am-I-doing-that choices). I even start a Pinterest board of ideas.

When I have the perfect challenges picked out, I open the notebook and across the top in big, bold letters, I write,

THE BFF SUMMER BUCKET LIST

1. Sleep outside

2. Best friend photo shoot

3. Face a fear

4. Get a tattoo (temporary—do I even need to clarify that?)

5. Canoe across Towne Lake (the long way—no cheating!)

6. Go shopping in pj's and have a shopping cart race

7. Break a world record

8. Random acts of kindness

9. Go letterboxing (also, google "letterboxing" to figure out what it actually is)

10. Host a fancy dinner (eating pizza on china and inviting siblings counts)

11. Have a water balloon fight

Rule #1: Both of us must complete every item on the list—together.

Rule #2: No taking the easy way out.

Rule #3: Challenge *must* be photographed for proof and bragging rights.

When Skyler arrives, at exactly 10:12, she's already telling me the bowling alley story before she's even in my bedroom. She does her trademark belly flop onto my bed, and I sit and listen to every word she says. I laugh at all the right moments and say all the things a best friend should say.

"And, Ella, Penny Boy totally saw the whole thing!"

says Skyler, covering her face with her hands.

"What did you do?!" I ask.

She tells me every single detail, and when I'm sure she's reached her venting limit, I give her what she needs to hear. "You so got his attention, Skyler. I bet he was talking about the cute girl with the gorgeous auburn hair the rest of the night."

Skyler relaxes her shoulders and smiles. "You think?"

"Totally," I say.

"Except boys don't know what auburn means," she says, giggling. "They never get my hair right."

"True. The cute girl with the reddish-brownish hair then." I sit down on the bed. "Okay, now I have something to tell you." I worry for a second that I've changed the subject too quickly, but her eyes get a sparkle in them and she leans forward.

"What is it?" she asks.

I slide the list across the gap in front of us on the comforter and cross my fingers that she'll be on board.

"A bucket list?" she asks. "Isn't that for things you want to do in your life?"

"Yeah, usually," I say. "But this is a BFF bucket list. And a *summer* bucket list. It's for us to do together this summer. You know, before high school." I wait for Skyler's reaction. Because everything depends on this plan working. She has to say yes. She has to.

She reads through the list.

She smiles. Good sign.

She laughs. Even better sign.

She points at the paper as her eyebrows arch up. Hmm.

"So are you in?" I ask.

"Um, this is seriously amazing, Ella." Skyler eyes me with a questioning look on her face. "But, *you* want to do all these things?"

I'm totally aware of what I'm committing to. And all the excuses I'll have to push out of my mind to get it done. *You can do this, Ella. It'll be fun.*

"With my best friend, yes," I answer.

"This isn't forty-seven scoops of ice cream. This is like, big-time stuff," says Skyler. "You sure?"

I nod like a bobblehead before I can change my mind.

"Okay," she agrees. "But there's one thing we need to add to the list." Skyler grabs a pen off the nightstand and writes below number eleven.

12. Speak actual words to our crushes

"Only one problem," I say. "I don't have a crush."

"Right," says Skyler with a mischievous smile.

"Like I haven't noticed your bike rides past New Boy's house on the corner?"

Oh, she's good.

"How could you possibly know that?" I ask.

Skyler stares me down like it's oh-so-obvious. "Okay, for starters, you couldn't stop blushing when you told me about the new neighbors having a boy our age. Plus, you get all crazy at the sound of a bouncing basketball when we're outside. And more than once you've bolted off the phone with me for an urgent ride to my house. And here's the kicker, Ella. You've been coming down Regency Court, which is totally out of the way. I don't need to be Sherlock Holmes to figure it out."

I bite my lip to hold back the school-girl smile clawing its way out, but I can't stop it. "His name is Alex," I say.

"Ooh, you even know New Boy's naaaame." Skyler smiles as she draws out that last word. "So, do we have a deal?" She sticks out her hand to make the pact official.

"Deal," I say.

We shake hands, do a little shimmy, and bump fists. Then Skyler rips a piece of paper from the notebook and makes her own copy of the list.

Well, now there's really no turning back.

CHAPTER FOUR

Skyler

1. Sleep outside

I AM NOT THE LEAST BIT SURPRISED WHEN Ella wants to start with number one on the list. I don't think I've ever seen the girl *not* go in order. I've gotten used to her lists and the rules that go along with them. Because that's what best friends do.

Although honestly, there *have* been times I've been ultratempted to rip one in half just for the freedom of it.

I open Ella's front door and walk in. We stopped knocking years ago.

"Hey, Ella. Ready for the campout?"

She's in the kitchen, surrounded by plastic contain-

24

ers, baggies, snacks galore, and a big red cooler. "Hi! I'm just getting some snacks together."

I pull a couple granola bars out of my bag. "Here, add these to the pile."

I was hoping we'd go bigger for this task than a tent in Ella's backyard—maybe with family camping trips (not that my mom would ever take time off) or tagging along with some of the other kids from school—but she had it all planned out before I even had a chance to suggest those things. I added "tablet with Wi-Fi" and "nail polish" to Ella's list of supplies though, so now we're both happy.

I plop my sleeping bag and backpack on the floor and climb onto one of the chairs at the kitchen island as she works. There's a stack of mail in front of me. I don't mean to snoop, but the corner of one of the envelopes pokes out to the left with fancy blue lettering giving the return address. I pull on the corner and slide it out just a little.

"Why is your mom getting a letter from Mensing Academy?" I ask. "Sorry, it was just sitting there." Mostly true.

Ella is rinsing grapes in the sink, facing the other way. "She went to Mensing back when it was an all-girls high school. She gets stuff from them all the time."

I push the envelope back in the pile and move it to the side. In with all the snacks is a big bag of Starburst—yum—but I don't want to mess with Ella's supply. I've never understood how sugary candy helps her stay calm instead of freaking her out even more, but it works. Maybe it's the chewing that does it.

"Can I help?" I ask.

Ella dumps the grapes into a container and seals the top. "Grab a couple ice packs for the cooler?"

"Sure." I pull out the freezer drawer as the phone rings.

"Hello?" Ella answers.

I drop the packs in the cooler as her end of the conversation gets more and more interesting.

"This is Ella. Are you sure you have the right number? Yes, Ella Wade. No, she didn't mention anything."

I turn up my palms, arch my eyebrows, and mouth, "What's up?"

Ella shrugs her shoulders. "Well, can you tell me what this is about? Yeah. Uh-huh. Okay, I'll ask her. Right. Bye." She hangs up the phone and scratches her head.

"Well?" I ask. "What was that?"

"I have no idea," says Ella. "Some lady asking if I have my availability ready for volunteering."

I reach for a container of pretzels and start loading

up the snack bag. "Did you sign up for something?"

"No. And when she realized that, she said I'd better talk to my mom first." Ella loads drinks into the cooler as we chat.

"Do you want to talk to her now?"

"It can wait," says Ella. "You ready?"

She's totally pumped for this. I am too, but I don't dare mention that I turned down hanging out at The Donut with Brooke and the gang tonight in order to do the bucket list.

We gather up our supplies and make two trips out to the tent. Our sleeping bags are set, our snacks are strategically placed between us, and a comedy is all loaded up on the tablet. We get lost in the movie, laughing so hard that we snort, and of course we tear up at the end. Ella even remembered to bring the tissues.

We go outside the tent to paint our toenails as the sun sets and the crickets chirp.

"We could sneak down the street and see if New Boy is out playing basketball," I say.

"Alex," says Ella. "But at nine o'clock at night?"

"Yeah, good point. Another movie?" I ask.

We scurry back inside the tent, and Ella loads up one of our all-time favorites.

"Wait." I take the tablet from her and go back to

27

the list of movies, scrolling down until I find the one I'm looking for. "Can we please add a little variety to our movie lineup?"

Ella turns to me like I'm crazy. "I told you I don't like scary movies."

"But it's not. It's an old one, and it's one of my dad's favorites," I say. "It's really funny."

"Skyler, it's called *Ghostbusters*. How can it not be scary?"

Ella is not easy to convince when it comes to a change in routine.

"And *you* seriously want to watch a movie about ghosts?" asks Ella.

It's so much easier to just let her pick.

"I can watch anything in a movie. They're totally fake. Real ghosts are scary." And trying one more time, I say, "See, it's listed under comedy."

I wait.

"Okay, fine." Ella pokes at the screen and presses play.

I snuggle into the sleeping bag and fluff up my pillow as the air cools a little.

The first scene is a little scary, but after that Ella is laughing along with the movie, which makes me happy. A little while in, it gets to a quieter, darker scene, and I'm now superaware that we're outside in a tent. Is it my imagination that sticks are cracking and voices are floating through the air?

"Did you hear that?" asks Ella.

"Yeah. You did too?" If it was possible to unwatch the scary movie from the other night, I'd do it.

We hit pause on the movie and sit up, with the sounds of feet hitting the ground and the crinkle of windbreakers coming closer.

"It's probably just my parents," says Ella.

"Or your brother," I say.

But the zip of the front flap makes us jump up and scream like little girls.

The top of their heads pop through the doorway first—blond hair and a brown bob. Brooke and Quinn light up their faces with flashlights and make ghostly noises.

"Did we scare you?" asks Quinn. She's smiling like that was the plan all along.

My hand is still on my racing heart, and I'm gripping the sleeping bag with my other hand. Ella is shoveling a Starburst into her mouth.

"Yes, you scared us," I say. "What are you doing here?"

Brooke inches her way in to what I'm now thankful is a four-person tent, and Quinn squeezes in behind her.

"When you said you couldn't come out tonight,

we figured we'd bring the party to you." Brooke grabs a box from outside and opens it up to reveal a dozen doughnuts oozing with glaze and colorful sprinkles.

"How did you get here?" I ask. We walk home from The Donut all the time but not at night.

"My mom dropped us off." Quinn still has an enormous smile on her face. "Don't worry, she totally checked with your mom before she left, Ella. You guys don't mind, do you?"

I turn to Ella, who most certainly does mind. Her eyes don't usually bug out like that. But she's too polite to say so.

What am I supposed to do, tell them to leave?

What I want to say is, "The more the merrier," but I tone it down since it's already supertense in here. "No, we don't mind. Right, Ella?"

Ella forces a smile. "Of course not."

We scoot over to make room for our new guests while I do my best to send Ella a silent "I'm sorry" with my eyes.

CHAPTER FIVE

Ella

2. Best friend photo shoot

OKAY, OKAY, SO IT WASN'T THAT BAD HAVING Brooke and Quinn at our sleepover. Although I'll have to crop them out of the picture we took for our proof of completing challenge number one. Brooke did bring treats—doughnuts no less—and Quinn is kind of hysterical, but two extra guests wasn't part of the plan. And you're supposed to stick to the plan.

We all slept in so late that before we knew it, it was lunchtime and everyone had to head home. But today it's just me and Skyler and number two on the list, a best friend photo shoot. So I'm loading up the cooler again for after-dinner snacks.

"Ella, what time do you need to be at the baseball fields?" asks Mom from the other room. I still haven't gotten up the courage to ask her what that volunteer call was all about, but I know I need to do it soon. Once Mom gets an idea in her head, there's not a whole lot anyone can do about it.

"Six o'clock," I call back. "Something about the lighting being best in the evening." Skyler's advertising mogul mom has put her top photographer on the assignment, and he's already given us tips on what to wear, how to do our hair, and what to put on our faces to bring out our best features. Of course I still don't know what mine are, but I made a list anyway, and everything has been checked off.

Mom strolls in the kitchen and must read my stare. "What?" she asks.

Come on, Ella. Get it over with.

"Why did a woman call and ask about my availability for volunteering?" I say.

Mom lets out a sigh, sits on a stool at the kitchen island, and pats the chair next to her.

"Mom, what did you do?"

She motions for me to sit and then puts her hand over mine. "Honey, I think this will be a great opportunity for you, so please don't give me a hard time about it."

Yeah, except she's still not telling me *what* I shouldn't give her a hard time about. Which makes me nervous. So I wait.

"Your dad and I think it might be a good idea to consider Mensing Academy for high school next year," she says.

"What? Why?" No good reasons come to mind. Zip, zilch, nada.

Mom is now rubbing my hand. "They have a great program, Ella. You seem to be very worried about the changes coming your way, and we thought a smaller school focused on academics might be good for you."

I jerk my hand out from under hers. "Mom," I say in as firm a voice as I can manage, "how is *more* change going to help me worry *less*?"

I know I've made a valid point when she pauses. But in her mom way, she skips right past my question as if she's already answered it.

"Mensing Academy requires ten hours of volunteer work each summer for students. They have all kinds of programs set up to make it easy to get the hours in."

I can't move. My hands are now glued to the seat of the stool.

Mom takes a piece of paper from her purse and pushes it over to me. "This is Cindy's number. Please

call her and work out a plan. We can talk more later."
Mom gets up and walks to the refrigerator.

Not one muscle unfreezes, but my brain is swirling a million miles a minute.

They want me to go to a new school? And a school without Skyler?

It's my hands that decide to go first, clenching into fists.

"I'm not going," I say.

Mom opens the fridge and grabs a water, not even looking at me. "Make the phone call, Ella."

And as she walks up the stairs, she shouts, "You know I love you, sweetie," like she didn't just drop a gigantic bomb in my lap.

Mom and I don't say a word on the car ride to Skyler's house, and Skyler makes it easy to stay distracted on the way to the baseball fields.

Skyler is still talking when she gets out of the car and goes to meet the photographer. I get out and shut my door.

"Call when you're done," says Mom.

I lean into the open window on the passenger side.

"Don't tell Skyler," I say. "About Mensing, I mean. I'm still not going, but I don't want her to get upset, okay?"

Mom nods and puts the car into drive.

I run over to Skyler and the photographer, who I soon find out is Eduardo.

"You girls have some ideas for the photos, yes?" he asks.

"A whole bunch," I say. I pull out my phone. "I made a Pinterest board of ideas." I'd spent the afternoon picking out all the perfect poses for us and putting it all together.

Skyler leans over and smiles. "Ooh, love the one with the feet. Which one do you want to do first, Ella?"

"We can do that one." I click on the photo of the two girls with "Best Friends" written on their feet in marker, make it bigger, and turn the phone around to show Eduardo.

He nods and fiddles with his camera. "Great. Let us start over there." He's pointing toward the fields beyond the baseball diamond. It's the perfect location with tons of tall, green grass and wildflowers scattered everywhere.

Eduardo pulls out a mirror and hands it over so we can get ready. Skyler has on a cute mint-green tank top with thin straps layered over a black tank, and a pair of jean shorts with matching embroidered designs on the pockets. She tucks her bangs behind one ear and flips her hair to the front on both sides. I'm going with my trademark navy blue in a short sleeve scoop neck and a light pair of jean shorts.

We race over and fling off our flip-flops. I have a Sharpie ready to go.

"You'll have to write on my feet, and I'll write on yours," explains Skyler. "Do you want 'best' or 'friends'?"

I pause and think about it, like it's the most important decision in the world.

"I'll take 'best,'" I finally decide.

We plop to the ground, and the instant Skyler touches the marker to my skin, I pull my foot back quickly. "That tickles."

"Ella, you have to sit still. This is permanent marker," she says, grabbing hold of my foot. "Don't move."

I sit through each letter like a good little patient, thankful I didn't pick the longer word of the two.

We're ready with our legs stretched out in front of us by the time Eduardo gets here.

He crouches down in front of us. "Now act natural. Let me see this beautiful friendship."

He snaps away as we giggle uncontrollably. I'm not even sure what's so funny, but I love every second of it.

"Show me the next one?" says Eduardo, and I flip back to the board of best friend photo shoot ideas.

For the next hour, we get in our poses and smile—running through the field holding hands, Skyler giving me a piggyback ride, the two of us jumping in a puddle so Eduardo can catch our reflection on the water. For the last photo, we make our way to the playground.

"You want the right or left slide?" asks Skyler.

I'm not sure why I'm just noticing she's almost always the one asking me what I want. Is that because I need to make the decision or because she can't?

"You pick," I say, and at that moment, I realize it's a little of both. Skyler stares at the slide and can't seem to make a choice to save her life, while I secretly hope she picks the right so we can keep the pictures consistent.

"I'll take the left," she says. And while my first thought is of the uneven pics we'll end up with, I tell myself a little variety might not be so bad. Maybe if I can prove to my mom that I'm okay with change, she'll forget about sending me to a different school.

"Great." I climb up the ladder and sit at the top of the wavy slide on the right, while Skyler climbs up to get in position at the top of its identical twin to the left.

But on the top rung, Skyler's flip-flop slips off her foot. She screams as her right leg comes out from under her and she lands hard on the rung. Thank goodness she hung on tight to the side bars.

"Are you okay?!" I head over as fast as I can, and Eduardo sets down his camera to get to the bottom of the ladder.

Skyler is breathing deep, not saying a word, and that's when I see the big, bloody gash on her leg.

"You must have caught it on something underneath." I lean down and hold my hands out. "Can you stand up?"

She shakes her head. "I don't think so."

Eduardo searches through his bags and comes up with a thick towel. He climbs up the ladder and wraps it around her leg. "I will carry you down. Put your arms around my neck." He picks Skyler up like a fireman and carefully takes her down the ladder, setting her down on a nearby bench. "We better get you somewhere to have that looked at."

I pull out my cell phone and text my mom to come pick us up ASAP.

"My mom is on her way." I really do think out my next words carefully, and while I know I probably shouldn't, I can't stop myself from saying them anyway. "When do you think we can come back and get the picture?" I bite one side of my lip.

Both Skyler and Eduardo give me a look. The one that says I'm a total lunatic.

"Are you freaking kidding me, Ella? I can't even walk," complains Skyler. "I'm not so worried about the picture right now."

I get the seriousness of the situation, I totally do, but this is our photo shoot day, and I really, really wanted that slide picture. It's my favorite. I wish we had done it first.

"Yeah, you're right. Sorry," I say.

Skyler's expression softens a little. "Fine. Let's just get it over with." She gets up on her good leg and drapes her arms around me and Eduardo to stand. Of course he needs to crouch down a bit to be even with us. We set Skyler down at the bottom of one of the slides and I sit on the other one.

"This will still be cute, don't you think?" I ask in an attempt to get her on board.

She purses her lips together. Yeah, okay, she's not very happy now, but she'll appreciate it later. I know she will.

"On the count of three, put your arms in the air like you just slid down. Ready?" asks Eduardo.

"Ready," Skyler and I say in unison, although one of us with a little more pep than the other. And we pretend slide, with big smiles on our faces. If Skyler was auditioning for a part in a movie, she would have won the starring role right there.

CHAPTER SIX

Ella

SKYLER MADE IT PERFECTLY CLEAR SHE IS
not doing the list today, with her messed up leg and all.
So I figure I might as well get some of the volunteering
over with.

"I'm still not going to Mensing," I say to Mom as
she drops me off in front of the animal shelter.

No way. Nuh-uh.

"But volunteering might not be so bad," I add to
stay on her good side.

Mom just smiles, which makes me nervous. If she
thought there was a fight here, she'd be throwing out

her best arguments. But that smile means she thinks she's already won.

"I'll pick you up in a couple hours," she says. "Have fun."

I walk through the doors under the SPCA sign and a woman with long, blond hair greets me. "You must be Ella. We're so happy to have you here."

My senses go overboard with the smell of animals and all kinds of yips, yaps, and meows.

The woman guides me to a little table near the front counter and hands me some paperwork. "I need you to fill these out, and we'll get you right in there with the others from Mensing."

Oh right. I forgot this was a group thing.

I'd never admit it to Mom, but I'm actually kind of excited for this, despite the nervous flutter in my stomach. We've never had pets (Mom says it's Dad's allergies; Dad says Mom is afraid of them), so this is my chance to play. I'm hoping for the little kittens, or maybe I'll get to walk the dogs.

But no.

Turns out it's clean-the-cages day. Ugh.

There's one girl in the feline room when I get there. She's short, with beautiful, shiny, dark hair that curls all over the place as it gets to her shoulders.

"Hi." She reaches out her hand and gives mine an energetic shake. "I'm Kaliyah, but everyone calls me Kali." She says it like collie the dog, not Cali the state.

"Hi, Kali. I'm Ella."

It's like the energy inside Kali is ready to burst out of her. "It's so great to see another girl in here today. I've been working with Mr. Cray Cray the last half hour and he's driving me batty, you know?"

I'm not sure if I'm actually supposed to answer, since I don't know.

"Sorry, with who?" I ask.

"The other kid they have assigned here today. You'll see what I mean." Kali hands me a spray bottle and a cloth and then points to the nearest cage. "You're lucky. I already did the poop-removal. You're on wipe-down duty."

I open up the empty crate, prepared to clean in silence, but Kali clearly isn't the silent type. She talks about everything from cat poop to Ivy League colleges in the thirty minutes we're in there.

"But enough about me. What's your story, Ella?" asks Kali. "I bet you're really smart, right?" She keeps on going before I can even respond. "You look really smart. So are your parents making you go to Mensing?"

This time I sneak in an answer. "I'm not actually going there. I'm only doing this to get my mom off my back about it. My best friend, Skyler, is going to Jefferson High, so I am too."

The door creaks open, and I inch myself out of the cage I'm bent into.

"Those dogs can really mess up a place. Is that cray cray or what?" the boy asks.

I don't even need to turn around to know who it is. I even try *not* to turn around, but I've spent enough time at Skyler's for her next door neighbor to recognize me right away.

"Ella, is that you?" asks Travis.

"Hi, Travis." I stand up and blow a piece of hair out of my eyes. "What are you doing here?"

"Funny story," he says.

CHAPTER SEVEN

Skyler

OH BOY MY LEG HURTS. ELLA ALREADY asked me this morning if I was up for the list today, and I gave her a big fat *no way*. All I want to do is lie in bed and sleep.

But at noon, my cell phone beeps. A text from Brooke.

I'm coming over with feel-better supplies! ☺

I text back a "no, thanks," but she doesn't respond. I even try calling to make sure she knows it's not a good time, but it goes to voice mail.

"Brooke, I'm really not feeling good. Seriously, thanks for thinking of me, but my leg is a mess, and I'm not up for company. Call me later, okay? Bye."

I snuggle back under the covers, my comfy pj's making me feel at least a little better, and close my eyes. When the beep from my phone goes off again, I sit straight up and turn toward the clock. I've only been asleep for twenty minutes and there's another text from Brooke.

Sorry. Just got your voice mail, but I'm standing on your front porch. Let me in?

The doorbell rings, and Dad's voice echoes up the stairs. "Skyler," he calls. "We're you expecting visitors?"

Visitors? Plural?

Within seconds there are feet stomping up the stairs and multiple voices laughing and talking.

There's no time to change (not that I could get out of bed if I tried) or brush my teeth, so I settle for a quick drink of water, which I swish around in my mouth. I smooth out my hair and wipe at my eyes.

And there's Brooke standing in the doorway with a basket full of nail polish. Quinn is standing behind her.

"How are you?" asks Quinn. She maneuvers her way past Brooke to my side.

45

"I'm okay," I say. "It's sore. That's all."

Brooke settles in at my desk, plopping her basket down and pulling out a bottle of nail polish remover.

I scoot myself back and take the blanket off my legs, pulling my feet out. The bandage on my leg needs to be changed and while I assume I'll have to drag myself to the bathroom, Quinn surprises me by offering to take care of it.

"I want to be a doctor someday," she says. "Or a vet. Ooh, or maybe an Olympian." She gets this far off look in her eyes and a smile on her face. I'm sensing she's the dreamer in the group.

Once my leg is taken care of, we get to work painting our toes. Brooke goes for the glitter polish, and Quinn applies little heart appliques to hers. I pick mint green, to match the colors of my flip-flops of course.

Quinn goes a little crazy with pictures, announcing she's posting them to Instantpic for all the world to see. And while at first it seems harmless, I suddenly wonder if Ella will see them. Does she even follow Brooke? And maybe more important, does she know my toes well enough to pick them out of a toe lineup?

CHAPTER EIGHT

Skyler

3. Face a fear

IT'S BEEN TWO DAYS SINCE THE PHOTO
shoot that put me in bed, watching nonstop reruns,
and every single day, Ella asks if I'm ready for number three on the list. She's been all kinds of mysterious
about what she's been doing in the meantime, but then
again, I guess I have too. Ella hasn't mentioned the toe
pics Brooke put out there, and I figure it's better not to
mention I've had company.

In a way, this leg thing has helped me put off my
least favorite item—facing a fear. But I can't hold Ella
off any longer. Plus, I do feel a little guilty I blew her
off and basically had an impromptu spa party instead of

hanging out with her. So after the girls left the other day, I focused on the list. Lucky me, I've had plenty of time to do some research on how to actually conquer your fears.

My dad welcomes Ella inside with a booming "hello there" and she's in my room in no time at all with a list in hand.

"You look good, Skyler. How's the leg?" she asks.

"Much better. It still hurts a little though." I sit up and scoot to the edge of my bed.

"So I made a list of things—" Ella starts, but I cut her off.

"You know, I've been thinking. Maybe a list isn't the way to go here," I say. Her eyes start to bulge a little, so I jump back in. "I've been reading up on it, and there are steps you can take to conquer a fear. I mean, I guess it is a list. Of steps."

With that, Ella's shoulders relax, and she sits down next to me.

"Like what?" she asks.

"First, we have to identify the fear." I grab a notepad and two pens off my nightstand, and then I rip a piece of paper out for each of us. "We both write down our biggest fear and what we think each other's will be."

"Okay. Easy." Ella starts writing immediately, and I jot mine down too.

"You go first," I say.

"Your biggest fear is anywhere spooky, and mine is"—Ella pauses—"change."

I knew she'd go with that, but as much as change scares her, it isn't her biggest fear.

"What did you write?" she asks.

"Yes, my biggest fear is spooky places, but no way is yours 'change,'" I say.

"What? Of course it is," says Ella. "I don't even like when there's a substitute in class. Or if the lunch ladies make tater tots when it clearly says french fries on the menu. I mean, that's just wrong on so many levels."

I have to laugh because it's all true.

"But what's the one thing you would never ever in a million years go near?" I ask.

Ella freezes and her eyes go wide. She leans back, away from me. "You don't mean . . ."

"Yes, I do. Say it, Ella."

"Nuh-uh, I'm going with 'change' as my fear." She turns her paper around like that's all the proof she needs.

But I match her by turning my paper around. And there it is in big, capital letters that she can't deny.

COWS.

"It's not made up you know. It's called bovinophobia. And that cow really did charge at me when I was five," Ella huffs as we step out of the car and onto the farm. "I remember every terrifying second of it."

I pull a big, heavy backpack out of the car. Her dad pulls over to a gravel parking spot to read his book while we take care of this.

"I know, I know. I've heard the story a million times. Like, every single time we pass a cow," I say dramatically. "Good thing it was behind the fence and you didn't get hurt." I've learned the best thing to do is to let her know I'm on her side.

We walk up to the farmhouse and introduce ourselves to Farmer John, my mom's go-to guy whenever she needs a real farm for a campaign photo shoot.

"Happy to help, young ladies," says Farmer John, turning to Ella. "Cows are over there in the pasture. Very gentle creatures, don't worry."

"Thank you. We'll take our time if you don't mind." I tug at Ella's arm to get her to budge.

"Not a problem. Call if you need anything," says Farmer John.

Ella reluctantly comes along, and I guide us to a

spot in the field near the cows, but not so close that she'll totally panic.

"Sit down and relax," I say. "We're on to step two."

The mention of a step relaxes her the tiniest bit, and I pull out the stack of books I have stashed in my bag.

"What's all that?" she asks.

"Stories about cows. Spooky stories. Books about fears." I sort them into three piles. "It's supposed to help."

Ella picks up *Click, Clack, Moo: Cows That Type* and studies the cover. I laugh because the main cow is typing on a typewriter with his hooves.

"Which book do you want to start with?" I ask.

She shuffles through a few and finally holds up a spooky one. Great, we're starting with me.

"Okay. Do you want to read or should I?" I ask.

"I'll read," says Ella. "Maybe it'll calm my nerves a little."

"Oh, almost forgot." I reach into my bag and pull out a package of Starburst, picking out a red one for Ella and a pink one for me.

She smiles and lets out the breath she's been holding. "Thank you. You're the best, Skyler."

We sit in the field for half an hour, reading book after book.

Moo! by David LaRochelle.

Scared Stiff by Katie Davis.

The Cow That Was the Best Moo-ther by Andy Cutbill.

By the time we finish the very last one, we're laughing and relaxed, lying in the grass and staring up at the sky.

"You can do this, Ella," I say.

She reaches her hand over to mine and squeezes.

We stand up and walk over to the fence, where one of the bigger cows is coming toward us. It walks like a cowboy, with a strut in its step. Now it's face-to-face with Ella like it knows exactly why we're here.

It leans forward a little.

"You okay?" I ask.

Her head bobs up and down in quick moves.

Nose to nose now.

Ella is stiff, and she stands straight and still, like a solid two-hundred-year-old oak tree. I stand close, just in case.

She takes a deep breath.

And that's when that cow decides to be a comedian and let out the loudest moo there ever, ever was.

CHAPTER NINE

Ella

OH. MY. MOO.

It has to have been at least two full minutes since "the moo heard round the world," and I am still shaking. Skyler is rubbing my arms and trying to get me to say something. But all I can think is *holy cow*, and I totally know how lame that sounds.

"Ella, say something." Skyler has a hand on my back now, and I'm pretty sure she's already said my name at least ten times.

The cow is still standing there. Staring at me.

I take a slow step back.

Then another one.

One more.

When I'm far enough away to feel safe, I stop. "I think that counts as facing my fears," I say, without turning away from his stare.

And I wait for Skyler to give the okay. To officially check this one off the list.

But instead, she says, "Pet it."

"Pet it?!" I whip my head so fast toward Skyler, I'm afraid it might pop off. "I'm not going to pet a cow! No. Thank. You."

And that's when I hear myself. And I laugh.

"What's so funny?" asks Skyler.

I push my lips closed to try and pull myself together. "I'm refusing to pet a *cow.*"

"I see that," says Skyler.

"I mean, a lion I could totally understand. A strange dog, sure. But a cow? Nuh-uh."

It's clear Skyler doesn't know what to do. All my life I've made her super-duper pinkie swear she understands it's a real thing to be afraid of cows. And now I'm laughing at myself for it. Eventually, she joins in.

"That was a seriously loud moo," she says with a laugh.

And just like that we're both bent over holding our stomachs.

I breathe in. Out.

I take a step forward.

Then another.

Before the last step, Skyler grabs my hand. "It's like petting a cat," she says. "But, you know, bigger."

I take one giant step like I'm Neil Armstrong making history on the moon.

At a snail's pace, I lift my arm, stretch it out, and touch my fingertips to the cow's head.

And I pet it. I pet a real, live, could-charge-at-me-any-minute cow.

This isn't so bad.

"Mission accomplished," I say as Skyler snaps a picture.

And as if Mrs. Cow hasn't messed with me enough today . . . she opens her mouth wide, swings her head in a semicircle, and lets out a noise louder than a roaring bear.

URHHHHHH MOOOOOOOO!

Skyler and I take off running—straight for the car.

"Who's afraid of cows now?" I joke mid-sprint.

We almost make it too. If it wasn't for the gravel taking Skyler down.

Hard.

• • •

"This is great," Skyler says as we sit in the exam room waiting for the ER doctor. "Remind me never to run on gravel again. Like ever."

I know it's not my fault, but I still feel insanely guilty. Skyler wouldn't have torn up her leg (again) if it wasn't for this bucket list. Although to be fair, she does have more than her share of klutziness. I mean she somehow manages to walk into walls on a regular basis, and the first day of sixth grade she fell over a seat in the middle of a packed auditorium. I could go on.

Skyler continues on her rant, so I sit back in the chair. "First I get a big ugly scrape, then a bloody gash that needs stitches. Stitches, Ella. I was supposed to go running with Brooke and Quinn tonight. That's definitely not gonna happen now."

I do a little head shake, breaking myself out of the trance I'm in. "Running? Since when do you run?"

Skyler stares at the not-so-shiny hospital floor and wrings her hands together.

"The girls want me to try out for the track team in high school. It sounds kind of fun, don't you think?" she asks.

The girls? No, it doesn't sound fun.

When I don't answer, she keeps talking. "I figured you wouldn't be interested. That's why I didn't tell you."

She's totally right. So why am I getting so mad?

"Plus, you do all that academic stuff," Skyler points out. "And you know that's never been for me."

She's rambling, and I still haven't said a word. I stop myself from asking, *So we're keeping secrets now?* Because I'm the one keeping a much bigger secret from her.

I'm relieved when a couple of orderlies make noise outside the room, giving us a temporary distraction.

"They keep those in the basement," one of them says.

"No siree. Not a chance I'm going down there," says the other. "Rumor is that place is haunted you know."

"Yeah, yeah, yeah," says the first orderly. "I've heard the stories, and I don't believe them for a second."

There's clanking and crinkling, and one of them pushes a big gray garbage can past the door. "You go down there then."

And as they continue on their way, orderly number two responds, "No way. You know, just in case."

Skyler and I are listening intently as my dad pops his head through the curtain. We both flinch.

"How's it going in here?" he asks.

We answer with, "Fine," and I hope he can't feel the tension in the room.

"Your mom is on her way over, Skyler," he says.

Skyler stiffens and her voice softens. "My *mom*? Not my dad?"

It surprises me too—I'm not sure I've ever seen her mom leave work before—but I do my best to keep it to myself.

"Your dad had an unexpected meeting out of town, and I have to go pick up Nicholas from his playdate," says Dad. "Your mom should be here in twenty minutes tops. Sit tight, okay?"

He slips Skyler's bag of books off his shoulder and sets it on the floor. "Thought you might need something to do."

I get up to give him a hug. "Thanks, Dad. I'll take good care of her."

Dad pats Skyler on the head. "You take it easy."

"Thanks, Mr. Wade," she says.

I sit back down in the chair and pull out one of the books from Skyler's backpack. Of course I get one of the cow books.

"I'm really sorry, Ella, but there's no way I can do the list tomorrow," says Skyler. "I can already tell this is going to hurt big-time."

I slip the book back in and pull out another one with "moo" on the cover. "It's okay, we can do it another day. The haunted house on Pine Street isn't going anywhere."

The next book I pull out is a spooky-themed one. Which gives me a very interesting idea.

CHAPTER TEN

Skyler

ELLA IS TALKING PURE CRAZY.

"I am not going into the basement," I say. "Have you lost your mind?"

"You heard them," says Ella, "It's haunted. We can face your fear right now and get it over with. We've already done the other steps."

I'm not sure which point to make first. "Ella, I can't even walk."

She runs out of the room and is gone for a few minutes. When she reappears, she's pushing a green wheelchair. She holds out her hands. "Ta-da!"

"No way," I say. "Are you freaking kidding me?" I shake my head firmly to make my point.

"Come on, get in. It'll be fun," she says.

I grab onto the sides of the bed. "I haven't even gotten my stitches yet."

"We both know those doctors are taking their sweet ol' time getting in here. They won't even notice we're gone," says Ella. "Plus, my dad said we have twenty minutes."

I let out an are-you-serious laugh. "Your dad said to sit tight until my mom gets here."

"Potato, potahto," she says. "Get in. I'm not sure how long this adventurous streak of mine will last."

I seriously do not want to be pushed through a haunted hospital basement, in a wheelchair, with an open wound that needs to be stitched up. But possibly worse than that is disappointing Ella, who is smiling like a fool and is clearly beyond excited for this.

"Help me up," I say.

Ella grabs onto my arm and guides me into the wheelchair. She turns us around and sticks her head in the hallway.

"All clear," she says.

But as she starts to roll forward, I put my hands on

the wheels and brake. After a quick glance around the room, I spot what I'm looking for. Or at least the next best thing.

"Over there." I point and Ella takes me over to the counter where I grab a reflex hammer and a magazine, which I roll up like a flyswatter. "Just in case it's more than a rumor."

"Good idea," says Ella. "That will totally protect us from ghosts."

She wheels me back to the door, checks the halls again, and races down to the double doors.

"You ready?" asks Ella.

"Ready." I smack the automatic door opener.

"Girls?" someone calls behind us.

"Go, go, go!" I whisper-shout.

And Ella turns on the speed to get us out of there. Maybe *she* should try out for the track team.

CHAPTER ELEVEN

Ella

WE DIDN'T EVEN COME CLOSE TO FINDING
the hospital basement before the not-so-easygoing nurse
caught up to us. She paraded us back down the hall, with
a very loud lecture about following rules and safety pro-
cedures. Which means Skyler gets to avoid her fear, for
now. But I have a plan.

The list is once again on hold, since Skyler is cur-
rently resting (and grounded), and my mom has strongly
suggested I think about doing more volunteering while
Skyler is laid up. FYI, it was not a suggestion.

Kali is waiting outside the animal shelter when I
get there.

"Hey." She waves. "I called your house this morning. Did you get my message?"

I did, but I chatted with Skyler for two hours instead of returning her call. What's the polite way to say that?

"Oh, sorry. I didn't get a chance to call you back."

Kali seems to take a second to decide if she believes me, but she jumps right back to her peppy self.

"Well, I requested kitty duty." She claps like one of those wind-up toys and even does a little hop.

"I take it you like cats," I say.

"Cats, dogs, ferrets, you name it." Kali loops her arm through mine as if we've been friends for years. "But kitty duty is the best, because we get to take them out and play with them."

We walk through the doors and up to the desk to report in. "Is anyone else here?" I ask.

"You mean is cray cray Travis here?" she says with a laugh. "He's on his way. We are apparently the animal shelter crew of Mensing."

I grab a pencil and sign in on the volunteer list under Kali's name. "I told you, I'm not actually going to Mensing."

Kali waves me off. "You'll change your tune after you see everything they offer. It's pretty awesome. All of my sisters have gone there."

"All of your sisters?" I ask.

"Yeah, I have five," she replies. "So I know. It's the place to be, El."

I give her a quick, forced smile since I'm really not in any mood to argue—about Mensing or my new nickname.

There's a basket of stickers and tattoos on the counter, and I leaf through it. "Ooh, Skyler and I can use these for the next thing on the list."

"What list?" asks Kali.

And like an echo behind her, Travis appears. "Yeah, what list?"

I'm not sure I want to tell them about it yet, and luckily I come up with the perfect change of subject. Travis still owes me a story.

"Hey, the last time we were here, you said you had a funny story about why you're going to Mensing Academy," I say. "But you got called out of the room before you could tell it."

"Right, right, right," says Kali. "What's your deal, Trav?"

"No biggie." Travis shrugs. "Just that my parents are always on my case about behaving and getting good grades, you know, stuff like that."

Kali and I both wait, but when she gets impatient, she pokes him in the shoulder.

"Okay, okay. Sometimes I can't help myself," says Travis. "I was taking this social studies quiz and the essay question was just cray cray. I figured maybe I'd get some credit for being creative."

"What did you do?" she asks.

"So instead of writing an essay, I made a comic strip. I mean, it was totally related to the question and it was hilarious, if I do say so myself." Travis stands tall and pushes his shoulders back.

"That's it?" I ask. "That's why your parents are shipping you off to another school? Because of a comic strip?"

Travis pushes his lips closed and his eyes get big. There's something he's not telling us.

"Spill, Trav. What happened?" asks Kali.

"Did I not mention the part about drawing Mr. Kleinman in his underwear and a *Cat in the Hat* hat?"

Kali and I shake our heads, cracking up.

"Oh, yeah. Well, I think that's the part that pushed them over the edge. The 'utter disrespect' and all," says Travis with animated air quotes. "But come on, it's always funnier in underwear and a wacky hat. Am I right?"

He's totally right. The three of us laugh so loud that the girl at the front desk asks us to quiet down and get to work. Travis finally signs in, and we all head to the feline room.

"Your turn, El," says Kali. "What's with this list? Tell me everything."

I guess since we didn't make a rule about keeping it a secret, I'm free to share what Skyler and I are doing. So I tell them all about it as the three of us walk around the small room. We poke our fingers in between the skinny, metal bars of all the cat cages to see who's in the mood to play.

"That's awesome," says Kali. "And no way can you just put a couple cat tattoos on for the next one. What fun is that?"

"I thought you liked cats," I say.

"I do," says Kali. "But every item on a list like that deserves to be epic. You know?"

"I figured because Skyler is home resting, and well, is pretty much grounded because of me, I'd make the next one easy for her." I beeline for the cute orange tabby. "Can I play with this one first?"

Kali nods and unlocks the cage. I'm guessing this isn't a new gig for her if she's been put in charge of a key.

"I heard about your adventure with Skyler in the hospital," says Travis. "I had no idea you were such a rebel, Ella. Nice." He smiles and nods his head like he's bopping to a nonexistent song.

"I'm not a rebel," I say. "And it wasn't much of an adventure. It didn't work out so well."

I take the orange kitten out and drape her over my shoulder. She instantly starts purring.

"You should go to the town fair when your friend is feeling better," suggests Kali. "It's going on all week. Go all out and get airbrush tattoos."

For some reason, this excites Travis so much that he jumps up, and in the process scares little Orange. I hold on tight and pet her to calm her down. "It's okay. Don't you worry your itty-bitty little paws about Travis. He's what they call a 'boy.'"

Kali and I giggle as Travis makes a funny face. "Whatever, ladies. This is one valuable commodity right here." He pounds his chest, but in the unmanliest of ways, ends up coughing from hitting himself so hard.

"Travis, do you even know what a valuable commodity is?" asks Kali.

"Of course not," he says cheerfully. "But it makes me sound all fancy and stuff, right?"

By now we each have a kitten in hand, and we take them to the little room that's full of fun cat toys.

"So it's settled then," declares Kali. "Town fair for tattoos. Is it okay if Travis and I meet you there for the big reveal?"

"Oh, um." I'd been so upset about Brooke and Quinn crashing our sleepover that it kind of became an unspoken rule there would be no more "guests" invited along. But having Kali there might be fun. Skyler always wants to hang out with more people lately (although not necessarily Travis), so maybe she'd even appreciate the effort from me.

"Wait, is this a thing that's like only for you and Skyler?" asks Kali. She must sense my hesitation. "Because I don't want to crash if it's your thing."

"No, no, it's fine."

I guess I've made my decision. "But, could you guys not mention the whole Mensing thing? I don't want Skyler to get upset about something that's not even going to happen."

"No problem," says Kali.

I turn to Travis.

"What? She doesn't even acknowledge me half the time," he says. "Your secret is safe with me."

"Hey, do you guys want to get something to eat after this?" asks Kali.

"I always want to get something to eat," says Travis.

The kittens are going wild in front of us, having the time of their lives. Just like I plan to do at the fair. But first I have some haunted house details to figure out.

CHAPTER TWELVE

Skyler

I'M BACK IN BED AND GROUNDED THIS TIME.
As big of a klutz as I can be at times I have never ever
gotten myself on bed rest twice in one week before.
Which, by the way, is totally unnecessary. But my parents are not very happy with the choices I made at the
hospital and seem to be going overboard with the con-
sequences. Ella says she's getting her own punishment,
whatever that means. I spend Friday night resting and
go to bed early. A Friday night in the *summer,* and I go
to bed early. Yeah.

I'm ready to do nothing but read and watch TV

today. When my mom pops in my room, I prepare for another lecture.

"Have any plans tonight?" Mom chuckles. "Sorry, that wasn't funny."

I'm not sure whether to fume at the situation or be happy Mom's sense of humor is around more often these days.

"What's up, Mom?" I ask, deciding I'm not in the mood for teasing.

"I know you're laid up, and grounded, but I also know you want to do some art classes." Mom stops and I wonder if she knows there's no logical connection here.

"Right," is all I say.

"I have some friends coming over for this painting party. Have you heard of those?" she asks.

I don't know what to respond to first. My mom painting or having her friends over. Who is this woman?

"No, what is it?" I ask.

"You get a group of friends together and the instructor shows you how to paint a picture," she explains. "You make a night of it, and you all end up with similar paintings."

I debate whether or not to ask who these friends

are that are coming over. Mom always goes out after work; she doesn't have her friends over.

"Oh, okay, well have fun." I open my book back up and push the bookmark into a spot in the middle.

"I'm inviting you, honey," she says. "Do you want to join us?"

"I, um, aren't I grounded?" I ask.

Mom waves her hand through the air. "Well, technically you're not leaving the house. Feel free to invite a few friends over." She turns and leaves the room, leaving me wondering if someone dressed like my mom was just in here.

But I don't hesitate to take her up on her offer. I text Ella.

> Mom is acting crazy. Wants me to invite friends to her painting party tonight. You in?

I don't hear back. Not after an hour. Not after two. I know Ella won't be thrilled with what I'm about to do next, but I did ask her first. I type in two more numbers.

> Hey, girls. Are you free tonight for a painting party? Don't ask.

Brooke and Quinn respond right away. They're in. They're excited. But, oh, they have to leave early for the party of the year at the bowling alley.

Great.

I manage to get up and get dressed, scoot myself downstairs, and get something to eat.

Mom's at work until the party, so Dad and I watch a movie together, and then I get to be lazy as he finishes getting things ready.

A few hours later, Mom's friends pile through the door. I recognize some of them from her office, and a few old friends I've known all my life. The others are new faces.

Brooke comes in with Quinn, and the party gets started with a superenergetic host encouraging us all to "release our inner artist."

I still haven't heard back from Ella. I check my phone for that "! Message not sent" notice, but it's clear it went through.

The painting party is actually a lot of fun. Everyone is laughing and painting, and the adults are drinking wine. By the end of the party, we have some pretty paintings to hang on our walls.

I stand with my mom, Quinn, and Brooke, holding

our masterpieces and posing for a picture as Dad snaps a shot of us.

"Put it on Instantpic," says Brooke.

And I do. Not even worried if Ella sees it.

Where is she anyway?

CHAPTER THIRTEEN

Skyler

I DIDN'T HEAR FROM ELLA UNTIL THE NEXT day with a big "I'm sorry" text that she left her phone at home and didn't get my message until late. And a couple more texts, Looks like you guys had a ton of fun and How nice that Brooke was free, let me know she most certainly did see the Instantpic photos. Although I couldn't tell if her messages were full of sarcasm or pep. Of course she gave no explanation of where she was all day, but I didn't bother to ask.

It's not Ella's fault I've been grounded *and* on bed rest for the past three days. Not really her fault that I missed an entire weekend of everyone from school getting together Friday and Saturday night. (Well, not Ella of course.) It's not *completely* her fault anyway. At least I got to do the painting party, and Brooke managed to sneak in a call to fill me in on the rest of the weekend.

I mean I should have been more careful on that playground, and I did run away from that cow and fall on the gravel. I didn't have to say yes when Ella wanted to go check out the haunted basement either.

Then why on earth did I agree to come to the town fair, on crutches, in ninety-degree heat? At some point, I'm gonna have to learn to tell the girl no.

"So how was it watching movies for three days straight?" asks Ella, fanning herself with one of the fairground maps. The guy at the booth hands her a long batch of tickets off the roll.

"Not as fun as you'd think," I say. "Although, get this, my mom stayed with me for an entire afternoon yesterday."

Ella and I had hardly talked at all those three days since I'd been grounded from all visitors and phones (minus the painting party), so I hadn't gotten to tell her. But I know she'll understand why it's such a big deal for me.

"Shut up, really?!" squeals Ella, in true, best friend form.

"Yup. She even watched a movie with me," I say. "I am not freaking kidding."

"Did she check her phone the whole time?" asks Ella.

"Nope."

"Get up to get a drink, but secretly make a call in the kitchen?"

"Not even one time."

"Whoa." Ella smiles, and she doesn't have to say a word. She knows how much this means to me. "Are you sure you're okay on crutches? I could get you a wheelchair."

I give her my best crazy look. "Don't take this the wrong way, but I will never ever, in my entire life, even if I live to be two hundred years old, let you push me around in a wheelchair again."

Ella looks like she's not quite sure if she should laugh or apologize.

"I want complete control over where I go today, thank you very much." I readjust my sweaty grip on the crutches. "Where do we go for tattoos?"

Ella's face freezes.

"What? I thought that's why we're here, right?" I ask.

"Yeah, but maybe we can do something else first and get the tattoos around six or so?"

Okay, there's seriously something off here. Why

does it matter what time we get our tattoos? And what exactly is this "something else"?

"Why six?" I ask, challenging her. She's obviously still uncomfortable, and I have no idea why. But as usual, I can't help myself from letting her off the hook. "Never mind. What do you want to do first?"

I wait on a bench trying to figure out what Ella is up to while she buys a blue slushie for us to share.

"Why do you have that look in your eyes?" I ask when she hands me the icy cup.

"What look?"

"Spit it out, Ella. You have some kind of plan." I take a slow sip, careful to avoid a brain freeze.

"You still have to conquer your fear," she says.

Oh boy, I was hoping our wheelchair race would someway, somehow count. I quickly choose another not-so-bad option. "Okay, let's go in the haunted house and get it over with."

Ella shakes her head. "No way. That's just high school kids jumping out of the dark for minimum wage and not actually being scary."

I'm not sure what she's getting at, so I wait.

"We're doing a real haunted house," she says, and I instantly know what she means. Pine Street.

"No way."

"You are not going to win this argument, Skyler. First of all, it's right there." Ella points to the old house in the distance, which sits along the edge of the fairgrounds. It's part of our town's history, with tons of spooky stories told about it over the years. It's totally falling apart, but no one dares tear it down and upset whoever (or whatever) might be in there.

"No way," I say again.

But Ella isn't done. "And second, I pet a *cow*."

Darn it. Petting a cow for the win. There's no use arguing this one.

"Fine, let's go," I say.

It takes much longer on the crutches, but Ella walks slowly, right by my side the whole time. Everyone is busy with the fair and the house is far enough away for us to barely be a blip on the radar.

"We seriously should not be doing this." I've changed my tune when we get to the front door marked DO NOT ENTER.

Ella reaches for the door handle like she doesn't even hear me. There's a loud *click*, and the door creaks open as it drags along the floor.

I grip the crutches, ready to use one as a baseball bat if necessary.

The house is dark inside, even though it's the middle of the day. Ella steps in and opens up a set of curtains, scattering layers of dust everywhere. We cough through it, and at least now I can see what's in front of me, which is pretty much old, broken furniture and a gross mix of dust, dirt, and unidentifiable substances. It's eerily quiet.

And it's not really that spooky. It's a regular old house that's no one's taken care of in a long, long time. It's not as bad as I was expecting it to be.

That is, until we hear a *CRASH!*

Ella and I turn to each other and instinctively run for the door. Although mine is more of a tortoise kind of run.

"Ella, get me out of here!" I yell.

But then she stops in the doorway, blocking my way. "Hold on," she says.

It's quiet again.

"Seriously, you need to move." I make my way forward until I'm right in front of her.

Instead of leading me out, she steps around me, back into the house. Slowly.

The floor seems to groan under her feet.

Ella reaches for a door that will mostly likely lead us to either a closet or the basement stairs. Oh heck no. I am *not* going in the basement.

"Ella, are you insane?" I beg her with my eyes to stop all the nonsense and get us out of this place.

"Skyler, no one has lived here in decades," she reassures me. "It's the middle of the day, and we're surrounded by a town fair."

Her words are not comforting.

"It's a haunted house. None of that matters," I argue. "And by the way, why aren't you freaked out?"

Ella shrugs her shoulders. "I don't like scary movies, but I don't believe that stuff in real life."

Funny, I'm exactly the opposite. Movies are fake, but real life is *real*.

"Skyler, you are facing your fear." Ella grabs the door handle, which squeals as she turns it, opening what I imagine is the way to a spooky old dungeon.

The only thing that appears besides the darkness is a bright green pair of glowing eyes.

And tiny, catlike pupils.

Meowwww.

A plump little kitty saunters through the opening and starts rubbing against my leg.

"See, just a cat," says Ella. "And from the looks of it, he's well fed. I bet he found his way in through a hole in the wall."

My instincts compete as one tells me to drop the

crutches and crawl out of there if I have to, and the other really, really wants to pet this cat. It's so cute. I give in and my fears practically vanish.

When I turn back to Ella, the house doesn't look so haunted anymore, just abandoned.

With a few more meows, the little kitten walks out the front door.

And with another goal checked off the list, so do we.

CHAPTER FOURTEEN

Skyler

4. Get a tattoo
(temporary—do I even need to clarify that?)

THE BANDAGED LEG GETS ME SOME SYMPATHY as people let us in front of them in line after line. Which seriously helps, because these crutches are starting to make my armpits sore.

We ride the Ferris wheel, the Tilt-A-Whirl, and every other ride in sight, except the ones I'd have to stand up in. We eat fried dough and kettle corn, downed by huge cups of lemonade.

Ella checks the time on her phone. The screen says 5:58.

"Let's go get the tattoos now," says Ella. She doesn't

wait for a response from me, just turns and heads in the opposite direction.

I stand still. "Um, can't go that fast, remember?"

"Oh, right, sorry." Ella waits, but she bounces on her heels like she's the White Rabbit in *Alice in Wonderland* about to be late for a very important date.

"Do we have an appointment or something?" I ask, struggling to keep up.

"I figured you'd be about ready to go home. That's all," she says.

The booth isn't that far, but after hiking around on a bad leg for two hours, I plop myself down in the nearest chair as soon as we get there.

One of the artists gives us each a few laminated papers with the image choices on them. There are rainbows and bunnies and skulls with crossbones, among a million others.

"What are you getting?" I ask Ella.

She points to a colorful butterfly. "I totally love this one. Don't you?"

"It's pretty," I say.

"Want to get matching ones?" asks Ella. "That would be so fun!"

I don't want to get matching tattoos. I want my own. But I know she'll be disappointed if I say so.

"Um, well." I flip the sheet and find a whole other set of images. "Ooh, I *love* this one."

Ella leans over and scrunches up her nose. "A dragon?"

Should I just go with the matching butterfly? No, Skyler, not this time.

"Nothing roars louder than a dragon," I say in my defense. "I mean, come on, it breathes *fire*."

"Okay," says Ella to the two girls working the tattoo booth. "We'll take the butterfly and the dragon, please."

One of the workers does my arm while the other works on Ella's. So far, this list has been more of a headache (or really a leg ache) than an adventure, but I have to agree the tattoos are a good choice.

"Those. Are. Amazing. Hi, El." A girl with gorgeous dark hair that's full of bouncy curls walks up next to Ella. "And you must be Skyler. I've heard a lot about you."

Ella reaches in her pocket and unwraps a Starburst with one hand.

"Oh, uh, who are you?" I ask the girl. But I quickly turn to Ella, waiting for her to speak. She stays quiet.

"Kaliyah. But you can call me Kali." I get a picture of a collie in my head when she says her name with

85

a slight accent. Kali holds out her arm and shakes my hand. "I volunteer with El."

"With *El*? You volun—" Before I can finish my sentence, another voice is behind me. This one I know.

"A dragon. Very cool. And also totes cray cray."

Travis.

"Hi, Ella. What's up, Kali?" Travis and Kali fist-bump, but Ella is still sitting there chewing her candy.

"I'm sorry, how do you three know one another again?" I ask since I'm not getting any information from Ella.

"We volunteer at the animal shelter," says Travis.

"You're all volunteering there? Since when?" I ask.

"We have to, otherwise Men—" Kali elbows Travis in the ribs. "Ouch!"

"Men what?" I ask. Something really strange is happening here. "Ella, what's going on?"

She's still panicked, I can tell. But seriously, what is up with her?

"I started volunteering at the animal shelter," says Ella. "My mom is kind of insisting on it. So I've been doing it while you were resting your leg."

I squint my eyes, trying to understand. "Why wouldn't you tell me that?"

Ella shrugs.

"Did you know we were getting tattoos?" I ask Kali and Travis.

"Yes," says Kali, "But we kind of invited ourselves. I hope that's okay."

I turn to Ella and I'm 100 percent positive she knows what I'm telepathically saying to her. *You gave me a hard time about Brooke and Quinn, but you get to invite your friends?*

"No, it's totally fine," I say because it's already awkward enough. "Seriously. Sit down and get a tattoo." And it really would have been fine, if Ella had just told me they were coming instead of acting like a total loon. Since when don't we tell each other the truth?

Kali picks out an adorable little glittery penguin that seems to fit her personality perfectly. Cute, tiny, and full of energy. I'm not surprised when Travis, the star player on the team every year, picks a soccer ball.

"Would you mind taking our picture?" Ella asks the girl when we're all finished. And I wait to see if she'll let Kali and Travis in the picture. I happen to know she cropped Brooke and Quinn out of the last one.

But Kali pulls Travis by the arm and takes a step away from us. "This is your list. I'll take the pic."

I can't help but like this girl.

Kali takes Ella's phone and snaps a shot of the two of us with our arms up, showing our shiny new tats.

"Ready to go?" I ask. "I'm pretty worn out."

Ella nods, and I prop myself up and grab my crutches. But when I turn around, I see him.

Penny Boy.

"We gotta go," I say. I turn as fast as I can and practically gallop toward the nearest hiding place.

The others follow me without question as I push open the restroom door and go in.

The heavy door swings closed and the four of us huddle together.

"Why are we hiding?" asks Kali in a whisper.

"A better question is, why are you in the men's room?" There's a boy at the far sink, washing his hands.

"We're not in the—" I start, but quickly I understand he's totally right.

"We're in the wrong one," says Ella. "We're not allowed in the men's room."

"*I'm* allowed in the men's room," Travis points out.

Kali bends down and checks for feet under the stalls. "It's fine. No one's even in here."

The boy reaches for the paper towels. "Uh, *I'm* in here."

Kali opens the door. "Not anymore. Private meeting." I'm starting to think maybe *she* should have the dragon tattoo.

When the boy leaves, the three of them turn to me.

"Okay," says Kali, "Who are we hiding from?"

"Penny Boy," I say.

"Penny Boy?" Kali and Travis ask at once.

"Penny Boy is here?" asks Ella.

I nod.

"He's her secret crush," Ella answers for me.

Travis lets out a sigh, like he was hoping for something more exciting than girl stuff.

Kali starts rubbing her palms together. "Ooh, fun. Let's go find him. It's on the list, right? To talk to your crushes?" She pulls the door open, and she and Ella poke their heads outside. "What does he look like?"

I close my eyes and smile. "Tall. Athletic. Gorgeous."

"Uh-huh, uh-huh," says Kali. "Not all that helpful, but we can work with that. Hair color?"

"Light brown," I say. "I think. I've only seen him from the side or from a distance."

"Great. Even more helpful," teases Kali.

"Uh-oh!" Ella clears us all out of the way and pushes the door shut.

"Oh man, what now?" asks Travis. "How much longer until we can get out of here?"

"Alex is here too," says Ella.

This time, *I* pull the door open, and Kali squeezes her head next to mine.

"Where?" I ask.

"In line for the bumper cars," says Ella. "But don't look!"

Yeah right.

"And what does *he* look like?" asks Kali.

"Like heaven." Ella sways side to side like she's in dreamland.

"Come on," scoffs Travis. "Is this really how girls talk? That's—"

And in unison, we all help him finish his sentence. "Cray cray."

Travis laughs and pushes the door completely open and holds it for us. "Can we please get out of here now? Crazy ladies first."

"Yes, but make sure they don't see us," says Ella.

Travis shakes his head. "I thought you were supposed to talk to them."

"No way!" Ella and I shout.

"What if they saw us watching from the bathroom?" I say.

"Good point. Let's get you out of here," says Kali, going all Secret Service on us.

And as if going in the wrong bathroom wasn't embarrassing enough, having to walk past a gaggle of cute boys heading inside seals the humiliation deal.

CHAPTER FIFTEEN

Ella

5. Canoe across Towne Lake
(the long way—no cheating!)

SKYLER'S LEG WAS PRETTY SORE AFTER THE town fair, so of course Mom encouraged me to volunteer yesterday. But Skyler's feeling better, so today it's back to the list.

I text back and forth with Kali, apologizing for canceling our lunch plans. I'm not totally sure if the emoticon sticking its tongue out means Kali is laughing or mad.

I've been waiting on the docks for twelve minutes when Skyler walks up. You'd think I'd learn I don't have to be on time with her. Just as she gets to me, my phone rings with a call from Travis. I let it go to voice mail.

"No more crutches?" I ask.

"My leg is feeling much better," says Skyler. "The doc gave me the all clear. Although, he did say to go easy for a few more days. Did you find Travis's canoe?"

"Yup, all set. Already checked in with the lifeguard too," I say. "And I swear, it's just me and you today."

Skyler kicks a few pebbles and keeps watch on her feet. "Actually, I thought maybe since we had so much fun as a group, it would be okay if I invited Brooke."

Wait, what?

I've been looking forward to spending time with just Skyler for days. But I certainly can't argue my case when I broke the rules too.

"Oh. I thought it was just going to be us, but I guess it's okay." I can tell she's not happy with my response. What I really want to say is that I miss her, but what does that mean when she's right here in front of me?

"Yoo-hoo! Wait for me," shouts Brooke as she runs toward us. "Phew. I thought I was too late."

"Nope," I say. "You're right on time." Skyler and I smile at each other, but it's a different kind of smile. And I wonder when it got that way.

We all put on our life vests, and I make sure my boating-safety certificate is sealed up. Mom made me take the course when we went to the Adirondacks last year.

There are boats everywhere today. Brooke and I help Skyler into one end of the canoe and then carefully take turns getting in ourselves. Brooke gets in the middle because apparently she's terrified of water.

Um, maybe this isn't the activity for you then?

Skyler and I paddle. And paddle. And paddle some more. But no one says a word.

"Uh, you guys?" says Brooke. "Is something wrong?"

Skyler turns her head back to me and I meet her stare, but no matter how hard I try, I can't read her face. I have always been able to read her expressions.

"Okay, I'm going to go ahead and assume something is up," says Brooke. "Anyone want to talk about it?"

What am I supposed to say? *Actually, I didn't want Skyler to invite you here?*

"Orrrr we can just finish this *superfun* ride in silence?" She stretches out the "or" and says "superfun" in a crazy voice.

"She lied to me," Skyler blurts out, completely turning herself around this time. I can tell she's angry. But she's also wrong.

"I did not lie to you. I just didn't tell you they were coming," I argue.

"Or that you were volunteering," she says. "With Travis, no less."

At this point, poor Brooke has turned sideways and is bopping her head from side to side like she's watching a tennis match.

"Okay, fine, I should have told you," I say.

We've stopped paddling and are now sitting in a canoe in the middle of the lake. We're silent for a minute, and I have to give Brooke credit for stepping into the ring.

"All right, all right, girls. Let's take a few deep breaths," she says.

We both take her advice—me mostly because I'm too upset to speak.

"Good. Okay, now maybe we can paddle a little and get closer to shore?" Brooke grips the sides of the canoe, and for the first time I see how nervous she really is out here. I suddenly feel bad.

"Sorry, Brooke," I say. I grab my paddle and stick it in the water, but all it does is turn us in circles because Skyler is still pouting on the other end of the boat.

"Seriously?" says Skyler. "Brooke gets an apology, but I don't?"

"Can you please paddle so we can get back to land?" I ask, still turning in circles.

"No," says Skyler. "Not until you say you're sorry."

Skyler is not the stubborn type, so why is she picking to be this way right now and right here of all places?

I lean forward. "I'm not saying I'm sorry. You say it first."

"Are you freaking kidding me, Ella? What are we, five?"

But Skyler and I never argued when we were five.

"Fine, I'm sorry," I say. "Are you happy now?"

Brooke's grip is tighter. "Yup, yup, we're all happy now. Let's paddle."

Skyler gets back into position. We move across the water in silence and make it almost all the way across the lake. We should be celebrating, but when we get close to the dock, Skyler pulls her paddle out of the water. She turns back to face me and sets the paddle in front of her.

"No, I'm not happy now," she says.

It takes me a minute to realize she's answering my question from ten minutes ago.

Skyler leans to her left, sticks her hand in the water, and stares me down. "Say you're sorry and mean it this time."

She can't be serious.

"Don't you dare," I say.

"Skyler, what are you doing?" asks a now-terrified Brooke.

But instead of answering with words, Skyler forces her cupped hand through the water and splashes me right in the face.

"You did not just do that." I lift up the bottom of my shirt to wipe my eyes.

"She did," says Brooke. "Oh man, she did just do that. Ella don't."

But I do. I lean to my right, get a good handful of water, and push hard.

"Ahh!" Skyler's hair drips from both sides as she blows a slow, controlled breath out of her mouth.

"Girls, please stop." But Brooke knows enough to duck from what's coming next.

Splash.

Rock. Rock. Tilt.

Splash.

Drip. Drip. Drip.

Splash.

Splash.

SPLASH!

I'm completely aware of the rocking boat. I know this is a terrible, terrible idea. But I can't stop. I won't.

So with one more stare down, Skyler and I both

lean to the same side and push hard through the water.

But we lean too far.

Way too far.

We all drop into the water and the canoe flips over.

Bottoms up.

I break through the surface of the water.

I can't see Skyler or Brooke.

"Are you guys okay?" I shout.

Brooke appears near the middle of the boat and is completely flipping out, screaming and flailing her arms and dunking under water. I head over to her and shout for Skyler.

"I'm over here," she says from the other end of the boat.

"I can't swim! I can't swim!" Brooke keeps repeating.

"Brooke, we're in four feet of water," I say calmly. "Put your feet down."

Once she realizes she's not in any danger, she turns to me and Skyler. "You guys are insane. You know that?"

I bite my lip because I know laughter is really inappropriate right now. I glance at Skyler who is doing the same thing.

Brooke trudges through the water toward the shore.

"You're not going to help us?" Skyler shouts with a giggle.

Brooke shakes her soaking wet head back and forth as she stomps onto the rocky beach. The lifeguard is already there and hands her a towel as I give him a thumbs-up to let him know we're okay.

"We have to flip the canoe over," I say. "You ready?"

"Yeah." Skyler grabs on to the side, and we both give it a big push to get it upright. We drag it back to shore, but I stop before we get there.

"I'm sorry, Skyler. I really am."

She nods. "I know. Me too."

And right there in the water, I hug my best friend.

"Might be a good time to go shopping in our pj's," I say.

"How come?" she asks.

"That's all I have packed in my bag for your house. I figured I'd just wear them home tomorrow."

Skyler reaches in her pocket. "Yeah, plus, I'm gonna need to spend what's left of my allowance on a new phone."

And I sigh. Because my phone is in my pocket too.

CHAPTER SIXTEEN

Skyler

6. Go shopping in pj's and have a shopping cart race

BROOKE HAS ALREADY TAKEN OFF, SO ELLA
and I do the ten-minute walk to my house so we can
change into pajamas.

"Are you sure you don't want to get into regular
clothes and skip the store tonight?" I ask Ella. Although
I hope she still wants to go. I've been looking forward
to this item on the list. Shopping, pj's, and a shopping
cart race? Superfun and very little potential for injury.

"No way," she says. "I mean, unless you want to
skip it." But she doesn't want me to skip it. I can see it
in her eyes.

"Let's do it," I say.

As we burst through the front door and head straight for the linen closet, I shout down the hall, "Hey, Dad? Can you take me and Ella over to the store? We, um, kind of need new phones."

But it's not my dad who's standing at the end of the hallway now.

"Mom? What are you doing home?" I ask. Because she's never ever home early.

"I heard Ella was sleeping over, and I thought maybe you'd want to order a pizza or something for dinner," she says.

If my mom knows how weird this is right now, she's not letting on. When I can't seem to speak from the shock of it all, Ella jumps in and saves me.

"That sounds wonderful, Mrs. Grace. We were just hoping to get to the store first."

The two of us are wrapped in towels, and it's like Mom finally notices. "Oh, sorry, girls. You should get out of those wet clothes."

"Wait," says Ella. "Can you take a picture of us first?"

Mom snaps a shot of us, wet and frizzy, that I'm sure will be real attractive.

She ushers us down the hall. "Go, go. Get cleaned up, and then you can tell me why you're soaking wet."

Once we're out of hearing range, Ella leans toward me and whispers, "She wants us to tell her about it?"

"Right? What's up with her lately?" My mom is a good mother, she is. She works really hard; she stays on top of my education (although it would work out better for me if she didn't know about my grades); and she makes sure I have everything I need. But the downside? She not only works hard; she works all the freaking time. It's Dad who comes to parent-teacher conferences. Dad who watches movies with me. And Dad who makes the popcorn when Ella sleeps over. This is pure weirdness going on right now.

Ella and I get into our pj's, which takes some explanation on the way to the store, but Mom actually seems excited to hear about the list.

"Pick out a new phone, Skyler, and when I pick you up, I'll come and take care of it," says Mom as she drives.

Ella didn't have the same luck with her mom. She says Ella "will have to learn a lesson from this."

Yes, lesson learned, Mrs. Wade. Don't have a splashing fight with your BFF in a canoe.

Mom drops us off at the local buy-in-ginormous-quantities store because if we're going to have a shopping cart race, we might as well pick the place with the widest aisles.

I spend exactly five minutes picking out a phone (I know because Ella has timed everything we have to do) and we head off to get our carts. I figure we'll go with the standard pick and hop onto the bottom rack of the cart once we hit full speed. But then I see the car cart.

"Ella, get in," I say, pointing to the large cart with the big red car attached to the front.

She shakes her head at me. "You can't be serious. I won't even fit in that thing."

"You'll fit," I say. I grab the handle and pull the cart out of its parking spot against the wall.

"It's not a race if you're pushing me around," says Ella. "We need our own carts."

She makes a good point, but I have a better one. "The list doesn't specify who we have to race with. Just that we have one, right?"

Ella turns in a circle. "And who's going to be our competition, Skyler?"

I spot a boy from our school over by the electronics section. "Hey, Matt. Want to have a race?"

His eyes go from me and Ella to the cart. "Seriously?"

Ella pulls on my arm. "Skyler, come on. This is crazy. You do remember we're in our pajamas, right?"

Ella stands next to me dressed in an adorable pj's set

with tiny purple hearts all over (and matching slippers). I'm decked out in blue, with a little butterfly on the front of my top, a sleep mask to hold my hair back, and bunny slippers. Yup. Bunny slippers.

"It's not any crazier than going in a haunted house. Or tipping a canoe in Towne Lake," I say. And without waiting for her, I pull another cart out for Matt. Ella squeezes her way into the car, crouching down and sitting sideways to fit.

We line up side by side at the end of the longest, widest aisle and glare at each other as if this win is for national pride or a massive amount of money.

"On your mark," I start. "Get set. Go!"

I push as hard as I can, but it doesn't dawn on me until now that not only did we pick the heaviest shopping cart, we loaded it up with even more weight by having one of us in it. But I push forward anyway and when I get to full speed, I jump onto the bottom bar and coast down the aisle.

Our competitor is way, way ahead of us, and I get an idea.

I stop the cart with a jolt and a big thump comes from inside the plastic car. "Oops, sorry. Are you okay?"

Ella sticks her head out and rubs it. "What was that for? We're totally gonna lose now."

"No, we're not." I grab an abandoned cart near the watermelon display.

Ella smiles and gets out of the plastic car.

"Plus, we never said how far we had to go before we turn around," I say. "Only where the finish line was."

"Brilliant. We can win on a technicality." Ella climbs into our new, much lighter version of a shopping cart.

We turn the cart around as Matt notices what we're doing and turns his too. But before we take our final push, he gets cut off by an older woman, slowly creeping her walker across the aisle in front of him.

Ella and I laugh as we turn, and I jump on the bar of the cart. But we're so concerned with speed that we forget to take steering into account.

Uh-oh.

I see the display in front of us, but it's too late to do anything about it.

CHAPTER SEVENTEEN

Ella

WE SOMEHOW MANAGE TO CRASH RIGHT into the pop display—a direct hit at the exact point where the tower comes tumbling down.

I put my arms in front of me to cover my head, then grab onto Skyler's shoulders and hop out of the cart.

It's not just one or two stray cans that go crazy. It's one after another, after another.

Pop sprays in every direction.

Up.

Down.

Sideways.

At least it's a clear liquid.

Never mind. I take that back.

A case topples off the top of the tower, smashing into the not-so-clear pop, which squirts right at us like a sprinkler on a front lawn.

Skyler and I run for cover in the nearest aisle and wipe what we can from our faces. She turns to me, and I'm guessing my eyes are popping out just like hers.

"What do we do?" I ask. I reach for a Starburst in my pocket.

Employees are running to the scene and an announcement comes over the loudspeaker for a cleanup in aisle three.

"Listen, as much as I'd love to walk out of here like nothing happened," says Skyler, "we both know we have to own up."

She's right. She's always the voice of reason when I'm panicking.

Skyler holds out her arms and her pajama top is now almost as soaked as our clothes were earlier. "I think it's kind of obvious who did it."

We shouldn't, but we giggle. A lot.

"Psst. Over here." Matt, our race partner, is at the other end of the aisle. We run down to him. "You're not going to turn me in, right? I mean, that was superfun, but I don't want to get in trouble."

"I'll make you a deal," says Skyler. "Take a picture of us, and e-mail it to me."

He nods.

"It's my first and last name at mail dot com." Skyler moves right next to me and puts a sticky arm around my sticky shoulders. We hold our arms out and smile as Matt takes the picture with his phone.

Skyler shoos him off with a wave of her hand. "Go. Get out of here before we all get in trouble."

He smiles and takes off, disappearing behind a stack of cereal boxes.

"Hey." A big, burly man stands at the other end of the aisle. He does not look happy. "Can I speak to you girls for a minute, please?"

I know these kinds of requests because of my mom. They are not really requests and the please is just a formality.

Skyler and I walk the aisle as if it's a plank.

"It was an accident," says Skyler.

"Right. The shopping cart race we saw on the video monitor, was that an accident as well?" he asks, clearly not wanting an actual answer. "Are your parents here?"

"No, sir," I say. "Her mom is picking us up."

But as we walk past the demolished display, step

108

over cans and puddles of stickiness, Skyler's dad is the one waiting for us.

"Where's Mom?" asks Skyler as we get in the car. I'd been wondering for a while, but waited for her to ask. "She said she'd pick us up."

Her dad puts the key in the ignition and starts up the car. "She got called into the office. Some sort of problem with her Italy account. She said she'll—"

Skyler cuts him off. "It's all right, Dad. Never mind."

It breaks my heart to see Skyler's expression change to disappointment. She hasn't said it, but I can tell she's been hopeful about her mom being around more.

"You girls are very lucky they let you go home without a punishment," Mr. Grace says in the car on the drive home. "But I expect to be paid back every cent of the damages."

Skyler and I are sitting on blankets in the back seat so we don't get the fabric all sticky.

"I'm sorry, Dad. We will," Skyler promises.

"Let's get you home so you can clean yourselves up," says Mr. Grace.

For the second time today we'll be changing out of wet clothes. Good thing Brooke didn't get invited for this adventure. She would have flipped if her fancy blond hair was coated with high-fructose corn syrup.

When we get to Skyler's house, she showers first. Once she's dressed, she comes in her room and hands me a clean set of pajamas out of a drawer.

"Oh, I figured I'd have to go home after what happened," I say.

"My dad talked to your mom," says Skyler. "I was listening from the hallway. He downplayed the 'incident' so it didn't sound as bad as it was."

"Well, that's a lucky break," I say.

Skyler's dad is always telling us stories of when he was younger. He and his friends got in all kinds of trouble in the name of adventure. But he always ends with, "Remember to do as I say, not as I did as a kid," and a wink. So I guess we're getting a little bit of empathy from him.

When the front door creaks open, we both know we won't be so lucky with *Mrs.* Grace.

"Go take your shower," says Skyler. "I need to talk to my mom."

CHAPTER EIGHTEEN

Skyler

I WALK INTO THE LIVING ROOM AND PLOP down on the couch. Mom sits in the overstuffed chair across from me.

"I'm in serious trouble, right?"

She doesn't even hesitate when she answers. "You and Ella are young girls, and you were having fun together," says Mom. "But you have to respect others' property. Be more careful in the future, okay?"

I nod, waiting for the real lecture.

But Mom gets up, walks across the room, and sits down next to me. "I'm sorry I couldn't pick you up."

Wait. No lecture, *and* an I'm sorry?

"It's okay. Dad was there," I say.

Mom fiddles with her ring and for the first time I realize that maybe Mom misses me too.

"I want to talk to you about something." She turns to me and grabs both of my hands. "I know I'm not around a lot, and I want that to change."

I do too, Mom. But I also don't want to get my hopes up.

"I have an account in Italy that needs some attention," Mom continues. "I need to go away for a bit this summer."

Well that didn't take long.

I scoot away from her and hug a throw pillow.

"I'd like you to go with me, Skyler," says Mom. "What do you think?"

I turn to see if she's serious. "I can go with you?"

Mom smiles and reaches out a hand to smooth down my hair. "If you'd like to. I'm hoping you'll say yes."

"Yes! Yes! Yes!" I throw my arms around my mom and almost knock her over onto the couch.

"I thought you might be a little excited, but I had no idea." She squeezes my cheeks together like I'm five. "I love you, Skyler. We are going to have . . . what do you kids call it?"

"An epic trip," I say.

"An epic trip," repeats Mom.

"How long will we be gone?" I ask.

"Well, that's the thing." Mom pauses. "At least the month of August. But if it goes well, it'll be a year-long project."

"Oh." It's like my body deflates as I let out one long breath. "So you'd be away all of next year?"

"Yes," says Mom. "But I won't go unless you and Dad come with me."

"Wait, what?" I say. "How can I go? I have school."

Mom grabs a folder off the coffee table. "We've been looking into schools in Italy and we'd enroll you for the school year."

I have a weird game of tug-of-war going on inside my brain. On one hand, I have to stop myself from jumping over and grabbing that folder. On the other, the thought of being away for a year is terrifying.

"It's a lot to process. Take some time and think about it." Mom opens up the folder, which is full of brochures covered in pictures of Italy's beautiful countryside and awesomely cool cities.

Whoa.

"No," I say.

Mom looks at me, confused. "No what?"

"I don't need to think about it." I ask myself silently if I'm sure.

I am.

"No way am I passing up a chance to spend a year in Italy," I declare, debating whether or not to spit out what I really want to say. I decide to take the leap. "Especially if it's with you."

Mom smiles like I've never seen her smile before and leans forward, squeezing me like she's never letting go. When she finally sits back, she wipes tears off her cheeks. "I have a lot of work to do before we go."

I nod.

"Go ahead and tell Ella, sweetie. I'm sure you can't wait one more second."

"Oh, um." I stand up and glance down the hallway. The water has been turned off, but the bathroom door is still closed. "Could we keep this between us for now please? I don't want Ella to get upset that I might be gone for so long. She's really into finishing up this list and all."

Mom gives me a long stare. "Sure. If that's what you want," she says finally. "But be careful about keeping secrets from your best friend."

Yeah. Don't I know it.

The word "hypocrite" comes to mind as I wonder how on earth I'm ever going to tell her.

• • •

So I have three weeks to complete the list with Ella. We have six adventures to go. Totally doable.

And while of course I want to spend every day with Ella before I leave (especially if I'll be gone for a year!) I wonder how I can do that *and* hang out with my new friends too.

By the time I get back to my room, Ella is already on the computer. She turns when I come in.

"How'd it go?" Ella pretends to bite her nails.

"It actually went really well. She's not mad," I say, and Ella relaxes her shoulders. "What are you up to?"

"Guinness World Records," she says, gesturing toward the screen. "The good news is there are a ton of things we can do."

I sit down on my bed. "And the bad news?"

"It takes up to twelve weeks after you submit the application to hear back," says Ella. "And we don't have seven hundred dollars to fast track it."

Well, I guess we could put it on hold until I get back. *But I can't tell her that.*

"So send the application, and we'll skip to number eight," I say. But I should know better. Ella doesn't skip items on her lists.

She takes a deep breath and lets it out. "The point is to do it this summer."

"But I want to break a world record. How cool would that be, Ella?" I lean forward on my knees. "So the list takes us a little longer. That's okay, isn't it?"

"Give me a minute." Ella taps the keyboard, doing all kinds of searches. She finally stops and sighs. "You're right. There's no way we can get it done this summer, and I don't want to change it either."

"We could put it on pause and decide later," I say. "What's next?"

Ella pulls my copy of the list from the corkboard on the wall. "Random acts of kindness."

CHAPTER NINETEEN

Ella

"WHAT IF WE VOLUNTEER SOMEWHERE?" says Skyler. "Or leave little notes on people's cars? That's random and kind, right?"

Since things have been going so well with her mom, I take a chance. "What about asking your mom if she'll help us?"

Skyler turns away from me. "She's busy, Ella. You know that."

"Yeah, but she's been taking time off lately, maybe—"

Skyler cuts me off. "I could ask my dad if you want."

"Sure. Yeah. But I was just thinking—"

She cuts me off again. What's with her?

"I have a suggestion, so hear me out, okay?" says Skyler.

Now she's up and pacing the room. I'm usually the Nervous Nellie. "What is it?"

"I love doing this list with you, Ella. I do. Even with all the problems we've had, it's been fun."

I don't know what's coming, but it doesn't sound good with all the prep leading up to it.

"But think about it." Skyler sits down next to me on the bed and crosses her legs like we're sitting at circle time in preschool. "How much fun would it be if we invited our new friends too?"

This again. "Um, not so much," I say. "I want to do this with you, Skyler. That's the whole point."

It's pretty clear we disagree on what the point of the list actually is. We stare at each other without saying a word until she finally speaks.

"Ella, listen to me." Skyler leans forward and puts her palms on my knees. "We're going to high school whether you're ready or not. And there *will* be new people there. Lots of them."

I'm not sure it's having the effect she intended. Instead, my palms get clammy and my chest tightens. Skyler reaches over, grabs a Starburst out of the drawer in her nightstand, and hands it to me.

"You're my best friend in the whole world. But—"

This time I cut her off. "But? How can there even be a 'but' in a sentence like that?"

"*But,*" she says with emphasis this time, "I want to invite other friends along when we do things."

I glance at the computer screen with the world record information. At the list next to the computer. Our list. For us. Me and Skyler. Not other people.

"I'd rather not," I say.

Skyler squeezes her hands into fists and relaxes them, and I know I've said the wrong thing.

"I have always done what you want. Always," she says. "But it's time I stand up for what *I* want."

Squeeze.

Relax.

Squeeze.

Relax.

"Wow," I say. "I didn't realize it was such a hardship for you to hang out with me."

Skyler lets out a sigh and stands up again. "Geez, Ella. Why don't you get it?"

The jitters are turning to a slowly sparking fire, and I can't control my next words. "Get it? Get that you're tired of me and want new friends?"

Oh, Ella, what are you doing? But I can't stop myself.

"I want to finish the list with you," says Skyler, calming herself down. And then she gives me a firm, "But we get to invite other friends too, or I'm done."

Did she just give me a BFF ultimatum? She totally did.

This so cannot be happening right now.

I wish I'd taken a minute to breathe. Splashed water on my face. Slapped myself out of this attitude I'm suddenly sporting. But no, I open my big mouth before I can think about it.

"Fine. Have your new friends. Have all your high schooly things. Have a blast." I gather my stuff and throw it all in my bag. I use Skyler's landline phone, since my cell bit the dust, and ask my mom to come pick me up.

Skyler just stands there the whole time and when I finally turn to her, the tear fighting its way out of her eye trickles down her cheek.

What have I done?

"You're leaving?" she asks in disbelief.

I don't want to, but it's too late to turn back now. "I guess I am."

Skyler nods and breathes deep.

And that's it. That's all we say.

I grab my bag and head out her bedroom door. For the first time ever, I'm scared to death that I may have just lost my best friend.

CHAPTER TWENTY

Skyler

IT IS SERIOUSLY SO WEIRD NOT HAVING A cell phone on me at all times. I wonder if Ella would have called or sent me a text if she could have. I sit on my bed, staring at the home phone. But it stays silent like it has the last two days.

I can't say I'm not a little relieved though. After apologizing like crazy to Brooke for the canoe incident, she invited me out with her and Quinn to a movie last night, which included a large tub of popcorn and a way-bigger-than-you-need box of Jujyfruits. After the movie, we went out to dinner, spent the night at Brooke's, and had a full-out pancake breakfast this morning, courtesy of her chef-in-training older sister. I came home and took a nap, as a tired girl does after an up-all-night sleepover.

When my doorbell rings, I jump up and head downstairs.

"You ready?" asks Brooke.

"Yup. Let's go." I say.

"Now you do realize the info I got might not be accurate, right?" she asks as we walk.

"Sure, but if it is accurate . . ." I trail off and smile. If Ella *had* called, I'd be off following her rules instead and I wouldn't be doing this.

When we get to The Donut, it's packed. "You were right," I say to Brooke.

She smiles and grabs my arm, pulling me inside.

"How did you hear about this again?" I ask.

"Quinn's cousin heard from her friend, who heard from her sister, who heard from her bestie," she says. "Somebody organized an Adams Middle get-together-ish thing for lunch today."

We make our way in through the crowd and get in line.

"So why isn't Quinn here?" I ask.

"Family stuff," says Brooke. "Do you see him?"

I do my best to scan the crowd, but there are way

too many people in here. All the tables are full, and kids are standing near their friends or leaning against the half walls if they don't have a seat.

"No, but there are like a million people in here," I say. "Penny Boy could be anywhere."

We finally get our turn in line and order our donuts—a chocolate for Brooke and a custard with chocolate icing on top for me. But Brooke orders one extra—a glazed.

"Who's that for?" I ask.

"You'll see," she answers with a cryptic look.

There's literally nowhere to sit, but we find some kids from our school and manage to squeeze into their little nook.

It's not until I'm biting into my doughnut, cream spilling onto my shirt, that I spot him. I grab Brooke's shoulder and shake.

"That's him," I say. "He's right over there in the green shirt." I point to a table across the room where he sits with a whole hoard of friends.

Brooke leans over and whispers to one of the guys we're standing with and hands him the extra donut on a napkin. But it doesn't get weird until the boy walks over to Penny Boy and gives him the donut.

"Brooke, what did you do?" I ask.

She smiles, and this time it's devious. "I sent him a donut from you. Adorable, right?"

"Um, no." I'm still holding half a doughnut in one hand with chocolate all over the other hand. These things are messy. "Oh my gosh, oh my gosh, he's coming over here."

"You are going to have the best meeting story ever." Brooke turns to me. "You'd better wipe that custard off your shirt."

I put down the doughnut in a panic and reach for a napkin, but the holder is empty. There's no room to move to get one off another table, so I do the only thing I can and take a swipe at it with my hand.

"Skyler, you're a mess. You have chocolate all over your face," says Brooke. "He's on his way over."

"I know," I say frantically. I reach for the closest thing, which happens to be the shirt of the poor guy standing next to me, Kevin from my science class last year. I wipe at my face, my shirt, my hands.

He does a little head shake and puts his hands out in a "What the heck do you think you're doing?" pose. But he seems too stunned to actually say anything. Which is totally unlike him—the kid usually talks nonstop.

"I'm so sorry, Kevin," I apologize. Penny Boy is less

125

than five feet away. "I owe you a shirt, okay? I'm good for it."

I have no idea if I've cleaned up enough or not, and no time to check with Brooke. But I glance down at my shirt to make sure it's not totally embarrassing.

"Hi."

I look up at where the voice is coming from, and Penny Boy is standing in front of me, holding the glazed donut.

CHAPTER TWENTY-ONE

Ella

I'M VOLUNTEERING AT THE ANIMAL SHELTER again today, and I'm still miserable and pouty. That is, until Kali can't take it anymore.

"You've been moping around here for two days," she says. "What's your deal?"

I haven't told her about the fight. "Sorry, just some stuff going on with Skyler."

"You do realize you have other friends who want to hang out with you, right?" she asks, not giving me a chance to respond. "I mean, I'm guessing you're only here because Skyler is grounded. Am I right?"

Kali is the happiest person I've met, so I'm surprised she's letting me have it.

"She's not," I protest. But I quickly soften my voice. "We're, um, we're sort of not talking."

Kali gives me the kind of look my mom does before she tells me to go to my room. "So we're the backup. That's plain rude, El," she says.

It's at this moment that Travis decides to come into the back room where we're organizing supplies.

"Hey, ladies. What's with the cray cray looks you two are shooting each other right now?" he asks.

Kali is quick to pull him to her side. "Trav, when does Ella talk to you?"

"Um, you mean like when we're here?" he asks.

"Yes, here," says Kali. "Does she talk to you outside of here?"

"Uh, that would be a big ol' negative," he says with a swagger, turning to me. "I called the other day, but you never called me back."

"I thought you pocket-dialed me by accident or something," I say, realizing I never even bothered to check the message.

"Nope." Travis puts his hands on his hips. "Totally meant to do it. Wanted to make sure everything was all set with the canoe."

I expect Kali to be pleased that she has Travis on her team, but there's a sad expression on her face. "I know you want to keep your best friend. Nobody is trying to take that away from you," she says. "But you do have other friends, and you can't keep blowing us off."

I take in everything they're saying and it hits me like a cartoon hammer over the head. "I've been such a jerk," I admit.

Kali's shoulders relax and Travis drops his hands from his waist.

"Well, I wouldn't go that far," says Kali, "But I'll give you totally oblivious."

I smile a tight smile, acknowledging my guilt. "I'm sorry, you guys. I didn't realize."

Kali reaches out and squeezes my arm. "You might want to rethink your policy on new friends, that's all."

"Yeah," says Travis, "because we're kind of awesome."

As I stand there, I see it for the first time. How having other friends doesn't mean there's anything wrong with me and Skyler. It doesn't mean it's a disaster that things are changing. Because maybe, just maybe, they could actually change in a good way.

The clock ticks ahead, and while I still have five minutes left, I have to get out of here.

"I'm gonna sign out early," I say. "But I might need a favor."

Kali grabs Travis' sleeve and pulls him next to her. "Whatever you need, El. We're in, right, Trav?"

"Yup, yup, we're in," he says.

"Great," I say. "I have no phone, long story, but I'll call you."

I'm in such a hurry that I don't even remember to sign out. Thankful I'd planned to walk home today, I head to Skyler's house instead.

CHAPTER TWENTY-TWO

Skyler

"HI," PENNY BOY SAYS AGAIN.

But I can't speak.

I don't know if it's because he is one million percent gorgeous and I can't take my eyes off of him or if it's because Ella isn't here.

"You have a little chocolate on your . . ." He points to my chin, and I wipe at it. I'm pretty sure that not only have I *not* gotten the chocolate off my face, but instead I've managed to put more on.

"This is Skyler," says Brooke, bumping her hip against mine to get me out of my trance.

"Hi, Skyler." He reaches out a hand, and I shake it,

realizing too late that my hand is also full of chocolate and now so is his. "I'm—" he starts.

And I'm all ears. I want to know everything about this boy, my potential future husband. But just as I'm about to meet the love of my life, a girl behind the counter screams and flames go up around one of the coffeepots.

The whole place is in a frenzy.

The fire alarm goes off.

The emergency water sprays from the ceilings.

The smoke billows from behind the counter.

And everyone runs. Or tries to run. There are a ton of people pushing their way to the exit, so it's more of a walk than run.

Brooke hooks her arm through mine, and we stay close to the group in front of us, finding the emergency exit despite the thick clouds of smoke.

Once we're outside, the crowd spreads, but it's still massive chaos inside. I grab the door and hold it open as people pile out one after another. Or really, however many can fit through an opening meant for one.

People are shouting, "The Donut is on fire! The Donut is on fire!" which has a really odd ring to it, and I can picture it on news broadcasts all over the country.

The fire trucks come blaring into the parking lot,

followed by police cars and ambulances that end up having to park in the street.

Brooke and I back up to the grassy areas as the water spray from the fire hoses hits the side of the building and the "frosting" burns off the roof.

I reach for my phone to call Ella, but I stop. Because not only do I no longer have a phone to call with, but I also don't have Ella to call.

CHAPTER TWENTY-THREE

Ella

I KNOCK AND KNOCK AT SKYLER'S HOUSE.
I even ring the doorbell a few times (new for me and
also a little weird), but there's no answer. I'm on my way
home when the fire engines roar past me, lights flash-
ing and horns going crazy. There's a cloud of smoke in
the air coming from . . . The Donut?

I make a detour and follow along the sidewalk until
I get to where all the commotion is. Crowds of people
surround the parking lot as the rescue crew works to
put out the fire. There are cell phones out everywhere,
with most of them attached to the ears of kids my age.

Could Skyler be here?

I reach for my phone and quickly remember there's no phone to reach for.

"Skyler?!" I shout, but my voice is drowned out by a million other sounds. The spraying water, the chatty crowd, the news reporters on the scene.

The Donut looks like a giant bite has been taken out of one side.

"Skyler?!" I yell again, this time pushing my way through the crowd.

I catch a glimpse of Brooke and call out to her.

She turns toward me and certainly can't miss me flailing my arms like a windmill gone bad.

"Over here, Ella!" she shouts. Brooke turns away for a second and then pushes toward me.

"Where's Skyler?" I shout as we get closer to each other.

Brooke finally gets to me and wraps me up in a big hug.

"Are you okay?" I ask. "And where's Skyler?"

"I don't know. I lost her in all this craziness," she says. "She was right next to me and then they made us move back and—"

"But she's okay?" It's all I want to know. *Need* to know. That Skyler is all right.

"She's okay," says Brooke.

The fire chief assures us through the speaker system on the truck that the fire has been extinguished and the building has been cleared out. He asks everyone to please get checked by the EMTs before they go.

Brooke and I scan the crowd, which doesn't seem to be getting smaller any time soon. We shout for Skyler. We hook arms to stay together as we make our way through. But we can't find her.

I think to myself, *What would Skyler do?*

"I have an idea," I say to Brooke. "But I need your help."

I cup my hands around her ear and tell her my plan.

She nods and we head toward the fire truck in the front of the building. Brooke asks the fireman near the front a ton of questions, and she gets him to turn away from the truck.

I hop up on the big steel step and push myself off the second step to get into the cab of the fire truck. That speaker has to be around here somewhere.

Ah. There it is.

I grab the walkie-talkie-like speaker, cup it in my hand, and press the button on the side.

"Skyler Grace, please report to the big red firetruck. I repeat, Skyler Grace, please report to the big, red—"

The fireman talking with Brooke signals his friend

who leaps into the cab with me and grabs the speaker.

"Is there a reason you're in here, young lady?" he asks.

Well, I thought the reason was pretty obvious, but okay. "We can't find our friend."

"Is she still inside?" he says in a panic.

"No, no, she got out, but we don't know where she went."

I get a stern look. "Not the way to find her," he says. The fireman steps down and holds out his hand for me. "Let's go."

I take his hand for support and step down, but it turns out he was wrong. It *was* the way to find her.

"Ella!" Skyler runs toward the truck like an Olympic sprinter.

She's okay. She's okay. She's okay.

Skyler pretty much tackle-hugs me, and I take a step back to stay upright.

"I'm so glad you're okay," I say, still holding on tight. "You weren't home, and then I saw the firetrucks and got worried."

Brooke joins the hug, putting an arm around each of us.

After we get our fill, Skyler takes a step away, giving us all some room to breathe. "Wait, you went to my house?" she asks.

"Yes. To apologize," I say.

Brooke takes her cue and makes her exit. "Hey, you guys, I see my mom, so I'm gonna let you work this out."

"I'll call you," says Skyler as she gives her one more hug.

"Bye, Ella," says Brooke. I wave and a fireman calls us over to where the kids are all waiting to be picked up.

Skyler takes me by the arm and pulls me to a curb to sit. "I'm sorry too," she says.

"I thought about what you said, and—" I'm ready to tell her anyone is welcome, but apparently it doesn't matter.

"It's okay, Ella," says Skyler. "Let's just do the list. You and me, okay?"

"But, I wanted to tell you—"

"Just tell me we're not fighting anymore and that we're finishing the list," she says, cutting me off again.

"Yup. Not fighting. Finishing the list." A flood of relief runs through me.

"Deal then?" she asks.

"Deal."

Skyler sticks out her arm, and we shake hands, shimmy, and bump fists.

I just hope she doesn't mind the surprise I have planned.

CHAPTER TWENTY-FOUR

Skyler

8. Random acts of kindness

WHEN I GET TO ELLA'S HOUSE, THE WHOLE dining room table is covered with stuff.

"What on earth?" I step into the room and my mouth drops open. There are baskets, toys, baked goods, books, and gift cards, just to name a few.

"It's for our random acts of kindness," explains Ella. "We're going to pass them out to the neighbors, anonymously."

"That's awesome," I say. "But where did you get all of this?"

Ella beams, and I can tell she's proud of all the loot she collected.

"Travis's mom made a bunch of muffins, Kali's dad donated toys from his store, and I called a few of the local restaurants and that used bookstore. Everyone was happy to help."

"This is seriously amazing, Ella," I say. "Where'd you get the baskets?"

She turns to the heaping pile of all different size baskets. "Rumor has it Mrs. Davidson's a bit of a hoarder, so I gave it a shot. Turns out she's trying to get rid of things."

I grab one of the baskets and clear a spot on the table, but stop and look right at Ella. She knows exactly what I'm thinking.

"Yes, I already organized it all." She laughs and points to my end of the table. "This side is for families with kids, and this side is for adults. They each get a tag."

She's even made adorable little tags that say, "Hoping this gift brightens your day. #RandomActsOfKindness #PayItForward."

We get to work with Ella taking charge of the adult side and me at the other end with all the little toys. The only time we stop is when I put on some music and we do our best to dance to the beat and sing the right words. I don't tell Ella when she's way off on the chorus of a popular song, because it's pretty funny to hear her sing it wrong.

When the baskets are done, we load them up in her brother's wagon and another one she borrowed from his friend. We roll down her driveway like Santa Claus on Christmas Eve.

"Hold on." I stop, and Ella bumps into my wagon. Oops. "How are we supposed to be all secretive if we're clearly the ones handing these out? It's not like we can race away."

"Hmm. Didn't think of that," says Ella. "What if we hide the wagons behind a row of bushes and carry as many as we can? We can go back and move them when it's all clear."

I nod, figuring it's a pretty good plan, and pull the wagon forward. We go a few houses down and find the perfect spot to hide the wagons while we deliver the goods.

"So, are we ringing doorbells or just leaving these?" I ask. I'm not sure what would be better.

"Well, if we leave them, we feel good about it, but we don't get to see their reactions," says Ella. "I say doorbell."

"But people hate when you ring their doorbell and take off," I say. "I've seen the older boys on my street play that ridiculous game."

"They don't hate it when there's a special surprise

waiting for them," says Ella. "We're not goofing around; we're trying to be nice."

"True. Good point." I nod again and scoop up a couple baskets in my arms.

"You take the four on this side. They're all kid baskets except the last one," says Ella. "I'll do the other side, and then we ring and run, okay?"

"Back to the bushes?" I ask.

"Yeah," says Ella. "Then we can see how happy they are to get their gifts."

We smile and get in position like we're about to run a race.

"Go!" yells Ella.

I place one basket on each of the four sets of steps as Ella does the same on the other side. At the last house, Ella and I make eye contact, and she nods to give me the go ahead.

Ring. Ring.

Ding. Dong.

Buzz.

Jingle Bells?

We dash behind the bushes and can barely contain our excitement as we watch. And wait. And wait. Not one person comes to the door.

"Are you sure you rang them?" asks Ella.

"Yeah, you?" I ask.

"Mmm-hmm. Definitely."

We wait a few more seconds, but it's pretty clear no one is coming.

"Keep going?" I ask. Without a word, we grab the wagon handles and roll down the street.

What we didn't notice from the bushes is the three little old ladies on Ella's side peeking out from behind their curtains, now watching us closely.

"Do you think they'll go get it?" asks Ella.

I shrug, hoping all our efforts won't go to waste.

"All right, four more then," says Ella.

We hide the wagons behind another row of bushes and repeat our last performance.

Eight more baskets.

Eight more doorbells.

Run and hide.

This time, we get a payoff when four of the eight open their doors.

"Here we go," I say. We wait anxiously.

Door number one closes with a slam.

What? Why would you do that?

Door number two and three give us a little something as two women poke their heads out, pick up the baskets, and head inside.

But the last one makes it all worth it. One little kid runs out on the porch and his mom bends down to read the tag. She smiles, hands him a toy, and scans the street.

We realize too late that our heads are popping out from the bushes.

"Thank you, Ella," she shouts to us with a wave.

"You're welcome, Mrs. Bishop," Ella shouts back.

We stand up and grab the wagons with a handful of baskets left to go.

"So much for being anonymous. Who knew it would be so hard to give things away," says Ella.

"Right?" I say. "Still, we should do stuff like this more often. It's fun."

Ella and I smile, despite our poor showing so far.

"Hey," an older woman shouts from down the street. She's walking toward us slowly. "What are you young ladies up to? What is this?"

I wait for Ella to answer her, figuring she'll know who she is.

The woman is in a nightgown covered with a flower pattern and lace trim. Her slippers are doubling as shoes right now, and her hair is in curlers. She's carrying the basket.

"Oh, hi, Miss McCarty. We're just giving out some gift baskets," says Ella.

Miss McCarty has caught up to us, although it sure took her a while.

"Little lady, I am not eating these muffins if I don't know where they're from," she says. "And I much prefer to get my books from the library at my leisure."

Okay. Not sure what to say to that.

"We were just trying to do something nice," says Ella. "We're sorry if we bothered you."

I reach for the basket, "We can take it back if it's a problem."

She wraps it tighter and pulls away from me. "I didn't say I wouldn't keep it. Who made the muffins?"

"Our friend Travis's mom," I say.

"Does she keep her kitchen tidy?" she asks.

"Yes, ma'am, she sure does," I answer.

Without asking, she trades her book for one out of the remaining baskets, studying the cover. "Thank you," she says, her tone softer. "Been a long time since any random act of kindness came my way."

She turns around and heads home without another glance in our direction. Ella and I give each other our "What just happened here?" faces, not sure if we should consider that a win.

We pull our wagons down the street, but when we get to our next set of houses, Ella insists I do the red house on the corner. I probably should question it, but I decide not to.

"Kid basket?" I ask instead.

Ella scrunches up her nose. "Yeah, I'd say so."

I put the basket on the porch, ring the doorbell, and run to meet Ella behind the big tree in the yard. The door opens, but from where I'm standing I can only see feet. Boy feet.

"What's going on, Ella? I thought Alex's house was down farther."

"This isn't Alex's house," she says.

And when the boy speaks, I finally get it. "What is *this*?" he says, clearly in on what's going on and playing it up. "A basket full of *free* stuff? That's cray cray."

I put a hand on my hip, face Ella, and laugh. Then I step out from behind the tree and walk up to the porch. "Travis, what are you doing here? This is not your house," I say.

"Nope. Wish it was though. These people love video games *and* have a movie theater set up in the basement."

"So, what, you're hanging out in random people's houses now?" I ask.

Before he can answer, Quinn pokes her head out the door. "Surprise!" she yells, throwing her arms in the air.

I lean back. "Wait, you don't live here either."

"No, but my cousins do," says Quinn, stepping out on the porch. "When Ella told us what you were doing, we thought we'd have a little fun with it."

Travis is busy playing with the toy plane he's taken out of the package.

I wrap an arm around Ella and squeeze.

"Kali and Brooke couldn't make it," says Ella. "But I tried."

I appreciate her effort more than I can put into words.

"How's it going?" asks Quinn. "Superfun, right?"

"Well," says Ella. "Travis is probably the most excited we've seen after seventeen deliveries."

"Yeah, I just met Miss McCarty," I say. "And I'm still not sure if she was mad at us or somewhat thankful."

"You guys did good, I'm sure. Can we help with the rest?" asks Quinn.

"That would be great," I say.

The four of us walk down the street, this time skipping the doorbell ringing and running. We quietly place baskets on porches and know that it will most likely make someone's day at some point. And that's enough.

When there's one basket left, Quinn makes us all squeeze onto the side of the wagon, hold up the basket, and take a picture. We deliver the last basket.

Task complete.

CHAPTER TWENTY-FIVE

Ella

9. Go letterboxing
(also, Google "letterboxing" to figure out what it actually is)

AFTER THE BASKETS ARE DELIVERED, WE end up back at my house for a snack. Travis devours an entire bag of potato chips before I can even get my hand in there to grab one. Lesson learned—feed Travis last.

In the middle of the conversation, Travis gets a text and a goofy smile quickly spreads across his face. He mysteriously sneaks off to read the message.

"What's that all about?" asks Skyler.

"He's been texting with Brooke," says Quinn. "She's always thought he was cute."

"When did that happen?" I ask.

"I guess she gave him her number at the bowling alley, but I just found out." Quinn says it like she doesn't care, but I can tell she's annoyed. "Apparently best friends don't have to tell each other everything anymore. Who knew?"

I casually look away from Skyler, and she seems to turn from me too. I quickly change the topic. "Well, we still have some things on the list to get done if you want to help," I say.

"Absolutely," says Quinn. "What's next?"

Skyler and I answer at the same time. "Letterboxing."

"Letterboxing?" asks Quinn.

"Yeah, we don't really know what it is exactly," I say. "But it sounded superfun. I'll figure it all out and make a plan."

I turn to Skyler and study her face. I can tell she's hoping everyone will be invited along. I'm not letting her down this time. "You and Brooke will come, right?" I ask Quinn.

"Of course," she says.

Travis pops back into the kitchen. "Hey, you guys need to check Twitter. Search the 'random acts of kindness' hashtag."

Our moms are taking us for new phones tonight. Finally. After the disaster at The Donut, they don't want us to be without them. But for now, we have to mooch off our friends.

Skyler and I lean over to see Quinn's screen as she types in the hashtag. The first tweet catches my eye.

> Found a special gift on my doorstep today. Baked a pie for my mailman to #PayItForward. Thank you. <3 #RandomActsOfKindness

"It's totally Miss McCarty," I say in shock. "I don't know if I'm more surprised she's happy about the gift or that she actually knows how to tweet."

We all laugh. I mean she even made a heart and used hashtags. I'm betting her grandkids helped her.

"I guess we did make a difference," says Skyler. "Nice call putting it on the list, Ella."

The list. My heart must grow five sizes when I think about how it just might save me and Skyler.

The next day, Skyler comes over and we research letterboxing on the computer.

Basically, people hide containers all over the world for other people to find. So cool. The container always includes a journal and a one-of-a-kind stamp from the person who hid it. They leave clues on special websites for other letterboxers to go and find it. You have to have your own stamp and journal too.

"What do we do once we find it?" asks Skyler.

"You mark your stamp in the journal and sign your name, along with a little note if you want," I say, half reading from the screen. "And you mark their stamp in your own journal, along with where you found it."

Skyler leans back on her hands on my bed. "That's awesome. This is going to be major fun."

"Major Fun," we say in sync, saluting each other.

My heart grows a million sizes seeing her excited about the list again. It wasn't that long ago I wasn't sure we'd ever complete it.

"We need materials to make the stamps, and everyone needs a journal," I say.

So I make a plan, and Skyler and I text everyone with the details.

The whole crew meets at the craft shop the next day to get the supplies, and I introduce Kali to Brooke and Quinn. Then it's off to Skyler's where her mom, yes her *mom*, helps us all shape the erasers with our very own designs into actual stamps.

Researching clues on special letterboxing websites is totally fun. We pick the ones we'll search for and then all go home to get our adventure gear. For me this means a pair of old sneakers, shorts, and a T-shirt.

The first set of clues is at the local park, which is an easy walk for everyone in the group since it's right in the center of town.

"This set has four clues leading to four letterboxes," says Kali, reading off the list of instructions I printed out for everyone. "Should we split up into two groups?"

We all agree with a nod. There are six of us, so it makes sense.

"Whoever finishes last buys lunch," Quinn adds.

We do a big group high five to seal the deal.

"I'll take Skyler and Travis," says Brooke, grabbing both of them by the arm and hooking hers so they now look like a chain link.

I take a deep breath. Travis she can have, but she is not "taking" Skyler.

"Well, Skyler and I started the list so we should probably be on the same team," I say. I move a step closer.

"You already planned everything else about today, Ella," says Brooke. "How about letting one of us decide on the teams?" But it isn't actually a question.

I take another deep breath and then try to decide how to answer.

Kali watches, and I can tell she knows what's going

on in my head. She's totally perceptive like that. I also know she's about to try to make this less tense.

"I think it would actually be really helpful if you and Skyler were on different teams," says Kali, "since you're the ones who know how to do this."

Kali gives me a wink and confirms that she's up to something. I don't want to, but I go along with it.

"Yeah, okay. Me, Kali, and Quinn will do the even clues," I say. "You guys will do the odd ones."

We agree on the split and break up to get started. When we're finally alone, I stop in front of Kali. "What was that about?" I ask.

Kali tilts her head to Quinn to remind me we can't talk in private.

"I don't care if she hears," I say. "Why didn't you let me fight for Skyler?"

Quinn looks on, but doesn't jump in.

"Ella, you have to give her some room," says Kali. "And besides, we're totally going to win."

"What?" I ask. "Why?"

Now Quinn smiles, and she and Kali bump fists.

"What's going on?" I ask.

"We're, like, experts at this," says Quinn. "I did it in Girl Scouts, and my mom and I go once a month to find boxes."

I turn to Kali. "Yeah, me too," she says. "Quinn and I were talking on the way over and realized we've even found some of the same ones. We already have our own stamps."

"Why didn't you tell me that when we were making them?" I ask. "Or at my house when we mentioned it, Quinn?"

The girls laugh. "You were so into being the teacher," says Kali.

"Yeah," says Quinn. "We wanted to be good students."

I have to laugh too. "But you haven't found these before?" I ask.

"Nope," answers Kali. "These are new clues. But don't worry, we'll find them."

"So, you're saying we can totally win this?" Without waiting for an answer, I add, "Let's go!"

CHAPTER TWENTY-SIX

Skyler

IN THE LAST THIRTY MINUTES WE'VE FOUND
exactly nothing. But Travis and Brooke are too busy
flirting with each other to notice.

Now I'm the one in a tree, doing my best to figure
out what clue number one means. I seriously should
have fought to be on Ella's team.

"Hey, can you guys give me a hand here?" I ask.

Travis steps toward the tree. "Oh, sorry. What do
you need?"

"I need a boost," I say. "I think the clue means it's
in this tree somewhere."

Travis helps me get up a little higher, but there's still nothing.

"Brooke, can you read the last part again?" I ask.

She fumbles for the paper in her pocket and reads. "'It's for the birds.' That's all it says."

"Is there a nest?" asks Travis.

I search the branches and finally spot a small bird's nest that looks abandoned. I make my way over.

"Yes!" I exclaim. "There's a container."

I manage to get the journal, and we do all the required stamping and put everything back where we found it. Except this time I make Travis climb the tree.

The next clue doesn't require as much searching or climbing, so it's a quick and easy find under a bush near the creek.

But when we get back to the picnic tables, Ella, Kali, and Quinn are already there.

"Aw man," says Travis. "How could we possibly lose?"

I give him a look that reminds him.

"Oh, right," he says. "Brooke and I might have had something to do with that."

The opposing team is giggling.

"Did you guys have fun?" I ask.

The tiny muscles in Quinn's jaw tense as she watches

157

Brooke ignore the rest of us and focus on Travis.

"We did," says Kali, giving Quinn a friendly elbow. "Maybe next time we can all work together on it. It would be even better."

Quinn stands up. "But you guys do still owe us lunch. You ready?"

"Travis," I shout to get his attention. "Come on. You're paying."

We pile into a booth at Three Scoops with our sandwiches, fries, and a gazillion little paper cups of ketchup. You wouldn't know it from the name, but they do serve more than ice cream.

The next item on our list is to host a fancy dinner, and since letterboxing went fairly well, I figure Ella might still be up for having everyone else join us.

"So who's in for a fancy dinner at my house?" I ask.

Everyone at the table raises a hand and shouts, "Me!" Except for Ella.

"Oh," she says, "I didn't know we'd decided on your house. Or our guest list."

Oh boy, here we go.

"Well of course we're on the guest list," says Brooke. "If my bestie, Skyler is having a party, I am so there."

If I'm sensing a sudden possessiveness from Brooke,

I'm a thousand percent sure Ella is too. Plus, she and Quinn both seem to be stewing from Brooke's comment. I do my best to calm everyone down.

"Ella's right," I say. "We have a lot to plan. I shouldn't have brought it up yet."

But Brooke doesn't let it go. "So we'll plan it with you. Right, ladies?" She turns to Travis. "And gent?"

Travis smiles like he'd say yes to anything Brooke asks. "Yeah, sure."

Ella pops a Starburst into her mouth. Uh-oh.

"All right, so we have some planning and a guest list to take care of," says Kali, "but what else is on the list that we might be able to tackle while you're doing that?"

If it wasn't for Kali in this group, half the time we might be sitting around in silence. The girl knows how to get things moving along.

I nod and lean forward. "Well, we had to skip breaking a world record," I start.

"We're not skipping it," Ella insists. "It just takes a lot longer than we thought to hear back after you apply."

"Right," I say. "Not skipping it. And then there's a water balloon fight."

Travis slaps his palms together. "I am so on that. This fight will be crazy."

We all stop and stare.

"Did you just say 'crazy'?" asks Ella.

"Yeah, why?" he asks.

We all laugh at Travis's complete obliviousness to his trademark phrase.

"No reason," says Quinn. "We're just acting cray cray."

And the girls burst out laughing.

Travis just shakes his head.

When we finally calm down, Kali gets an idea. "You know, there might be another way to break a world record," she says.

"Really?" asks Ella. "How?"

Kali tells us about a library celebration in Rochester where they're attempting to break a world record this weekend. "They want everyone to come," she says. "They need nine hundred and ninety-nine people to break the record."

I wait, but she doesn't say and no one asks.

"What record?" I ask.

"Oh, right," says Kali. "The most people balancing books on their heads."

Travis is the first to respond. "That is totes awesome. And easy, right?"

"It's a little more than that," says Kali. "The books have to be balanced a certain way and everyone has to walk at least six meters. At the same time. With the books on their heads."

"How much is six meters?" asks Brooke.

"Eighteen feet," answers Ella, like she didn't even need to calculate it.

"Well, that sounds fun," says Quinn. "Would it be okay if I joined you, Ella? I can see if my mom will drive us."

Ella looks genuinely happy to have Quinn involved, but she makes no move to include Travis or Brooke. This little group seems to be hitting some rough spots.

"That would be great," says Ella. "Do you know where I can find the details, Kali?"

Kali and Ella lean over Kali's phone and start searching for more information. The rest of us munch on whatever is in front of us.

"It's this Saturday," says Ella.

"Great. In the meantime, I'll plan the dinner," says Brooke.

It's stressing me out every time she jumps into the conversation. Does she not see she's rubbing Ella the wrong way?

"Thanks, Brooke, but I'll plan the dinner," says Ella firmly. "The list says to host a fancy dinner, and I can't host it if I don't plan it. It has to be me and Skyler."

Well, she has a point.

Quinn jumps in to break up the staring contest going on between Ella and Brooke. "Okay, I'll text you guys to let you know if my mom says yes to driving us to the library," says Quinn. "We can fit everyone in the minivan."

The original plan was to all walk home together, but I know it's my responsibility to split up Ella and Brooke right now.

"I'm gonna go with Ella. Do you guys mind if we take off?" I say. But before I get an answer, I grab Ella by the arm and we walk away.

"Thank you," she says. "Brooke was really starting to get to me."

"I know," I say. "But you don't have anything to worry about. Just let her help, okay?"

Ella relaxes, and I think about what she'll say when she finally finds out I'm leaving in two weeks.

I should tell her. But I can't figure out how.

CHAPTER TWENTY-SEVEN

Ella

7. Break a world record

QUINN'S MOM IS WAITING IN THE DRIVEWAY when my mom decides to drop another bomb on me. "Open house at Mensing is Monday night, Ella," says Mom. "Don't make any plans."

I give her a look. "What's the point? I am not going to school there." I say that last line with as much strength as I can manage.

"Don't make any plans," she repeats.

What more does she want from me? I'm doing the volunteering. I'm making new friends. But I am not going to a whole different school. Nuh-uh. No way.

When I get in the minivan, everyone else is already

inside. Brooke and Skyler are squeezed into the back. Great. Quinn is in the front, and there's a seat open next to Travis and Kali that I get into. I would have guessed it'd be Brooke and Travis in the back, but apparently she feels the need to make her claim on Skyler.

Everyone says hi as I strap myself in.

It's an hour and a half drive to the library, and while I expect us to be chatting the whole way, everyone brought headphones and iPods, so it's actually a quiet ride.

When we finally get there, crowds of people are outside. We take our books with us and sign in at the registration table where they give us our official numbers. I get 704 with about thirty minutes to go. They explain how we have to balance the books and how far we'll need to walk when they give us the go-ahead. The volunteers at the table measure our books to make sure they're the right size, and we're sent off to find our spots.

"Do you think we'll actually be a part of history?" I ask the others. I didn't think I'd be so excited, but now that we're here, this is really supercool. I move over next to Skyler.

"I hope so," says Kali. "I've always wanted to break a world record."

When the others start chatting, Skyler leans her head on my shoulder. "Thanks for making the summer bucket list, Ella. I can't believe you're seriously doing it all."

I laugh, making my shoulder move and along with it, Skyler's head. She wraps me up in a big hug.

"What's that for?" I ask, hugging her tight.

"For doing this for me," she says.

And without looking, I know exactly what she means. We aren't the same Ella and Skyler we were in kindergarten. We're not the same friends we were at the end of the school year. Things are changing, and we're not always going in the same direction.

"I'm doing it for *us*," I say. And with that, Skyler hugs me a little bit tighter.

By the time everyone is ready, the line along the road-blocked street has grown so far I can't tell where it ends. We must be close to breaking the record, but they're not giving us a number.

"We need everyone to stand on their marks," says a female voice over the loudspeaker. "Balance your book on your head, and please wait for the signal before you start to walk. We all need to go at the same time."

The signal is supposed to be a horn, which turns out to be a pretty bad idea. When an impatient driver, who clearly didn't get the note about the roadblock, decides to honk his horn, half the crowd moves forward—the other half doesn't.

I'm one of the ones who moves, but the person in front of me isn't.

My book falls off my head and clunks to the ground, along with what must be four hundred others. Smashing into the woman in front of me is only part of the problem, because the line behind me turns into human dominoes and topples over, catching my legs in the process and taking me down with them.

The head librarian tries to get everyone's attention over the loud speaker, but it's a bunch of muffled sounds with all the shouting in the crowd.

I try to find my friends, but I can't. Just Brooke, who is sitting on the ground, waiting out the craziness.

"You need to get up," I say, reaching for her hand. But she won't take it.

"I can do it myself," she says, and she pushes herself up to standing.

Really?

"What's your issue?" I ask her. I've had enough of this attitude.

"I don't *have* an issue, Ella," she says with enough tone to let me know she most certainly does.

"Why are you being like this?" I ask, not letting it go. "Why now? Because of Skyler?"

People are still trying to get settled around us, and the librarian in charge tells us we're going to try again in two minutes.

Travis, Skyler, Quinn, and Kali all get into position and must notice that Brooke and I aren't having a friendly conversation.

"Hey, girls, you ready?" asks Kali.

But Brooke ignores her. "Being like what, Ella?

"Like this," I say. "Like all of a sudden I'm in the way."

"Maybe you are," she says.

I swear laser beams must shoot right out of my eyes. "Skyler is *my* best friend."

"You guys, stop it," says Skyler, taking a step closer.

"Skyler makes her own choices," says Brooke.

Quinn quietly moves Brooke to her spot and takes one next to me. Kali, Skyler, and Travis rearrange themselves to make sure they're in between us.

"You okay?" asks Skyler.

I nod, doing my best to keep it together.

"Everyone, please get back in place," says the librarian.

The crowd puts their books on their heads (again) and gets in position.

"This time I'll be doing a countdown," says the librarian. "Do not go at the sound of a horn. Move on 'Go.'"

I move one leg out in front, ready to make the six-meter walk.

"On your mark. Get set," comes over the loud-speaker. It's time. "Go!"

The huge crowd moves forward and there are no signs of books being dropped. I hold my arms out to my side for balance and focus on the pink headband of the person in front of me. I think we're actually doing it.

Once everyone gets to their marks, the librarian comes back on with a loud, "Woo-hoo! You did it!" And the crowd erupts into cheers, with high fives and jumps all around.

"Unfortunately," she says, "we are just short of our goal by fifty-three people. But please give yourselves a huge pat on the back for being a part of this world record attempt!"

There are more cheers from the crowd, but not from me. I let my chin drop to my chest. "We didn't break a world record," I say quietly. It might not be a big deal to most people, but for me, it means an incomplete list. I do not handle incomplete lists very well.

Skyler comes over and puts an arm around my

shoulders. "I know you're disappointed, but remember we agreed the list could be adjusted."

I know she means well, but it's not helping. "This was supposed to be an epic summer, Skyler. You and me and the BFF bucket list."

"Yeah, and it has been, Ella," she says. "We're never ever going to forget all the stuff we've done."

"I wanted to break a world record with you," I say.

"Well, we still have the application in, right?" says Skyler. "Maybe someday we will."

Skyler gives me a shoulder squeeze and smiles, and I can't help but smile too.

"We might even get it sometime in August," I say. But Skyler is the one who looks down this time. "What's wrong?"

"Nothing," she says. "Just that September is fine too, you know? Or even if it ends up being next year."

And while it kinda seems like she's hiding something, I shrug it off, because Skyler would never hide anything from me. I'm the one who's hiding something from her.

CHAPTER TWENTY-EIGHT

Skyler

QUINN'S MOM DROPS ME OFF, AND BROOKE insists on staying for a bit. Quinn plays it off like she's really tired and didn't just get totally blown off by her best friend.

"That wasn't cool, Brooke," I say as we walk toward the house. "You really should have invited Quinn."

"You heard her," she says. "She's tired."

I have to admit I haven't been thrilled with her subtle digs at Ella lately. And now she's being rude to her BFF. I'm not sure where it's coming from, but I plan on calling her out on it.

Before I can say anything else, my mom meets us at the door. "Hi, girls. Have fun?" she asks.

"Yes, Mrs. Grace," says Brooke.

"But we missed the record by fifty-three people," I add with a pout.

Mom opens the door and steps aside to let us in. "Well, at least you have a story to tell. Skyler, can I talk to you?"

Brooke points to the kitchen. "I'll go get a drink if that's okay."

Mom nods. "We'll just be a minute."

I follow her into the living room, and we both sit down on the couch.

"We have a week free while we're in Italy," says Mom. "I wanted to get your opinion on a side trip."

I peek through the entrance to make sure we're still alone. "Like in Italy or somewhere else?" I ask.

"Wherever you want," says Mom. She actually looks excited about this. Not just the trip, but us doing it together.

I want to tell Ella so badly. She'll understand. But then again, she won't.

"So we could go to Paris or maybe Athens?" I ask.

"Sure," says Mom.

"Or what about Venice or Florence?" I get more and more excited with each city.

"All up for grabs," she says.

"Hmm. I don't know, Mom," I say. "There are so many places to choose from. Can I think about it?"

"Sure, sure, sure," she says, patting me on the knee. "Just wanted to throw it out there. We have time."

"We leave in a little over a week," I say.

"It's at the end of the trip. We can always take a train somewhere last minute or hop on a cruise. And then if we need to, we'll come home to pack up for the move." Mom gives me a big hug. "I'm so thrilled you're coming with me."

And as much as I love this hug right now, and my mom's enthusiasm, my stomach clenches when Brooke pokes her head around the corner and smiles at me.

How much did she hear?

"I should get back to Brooke," I say, and I head toward the kitchen.

As soon as I get there, Brooke claps her hands. "Oh my god, Skyler, you're going to Europe?!"

I guess she heard a lot.

Despite me being annoyed, I couldn't help but get excited. "My mom has business over there, and she wants me to go with her," I explain.

"That's amazing! You're going to have such an incredible time." Brooke stops and stares at me. "Wait, why was your mom talking about packing for a move?"

Darn it. She heard *everything*.

I'd really rather not tell her, but I don't have a choice. "If she gets the account, we're moving to Italy for a year," I admit.

"What?!" Brooke takes a step back. "A whole year?"

"Yeah. I'd go to school there," I say.

"And you're okay with this?" she asks.

I nod. It does feel good to finally talk about it with someone, but I find myself missing Ella.

"Why didn't you tell me?" asks Brooke. "Wait, does Ella know?"

I look down and shake my head. "No, I'm kind of afraid to tell her."

"What? Why? She should be thrilled for you," says Brooke. "I mean, I'm totally gonna miss you, but I expect all kinds of pictures of cute Italian boys on a daily basis."

I laugh. "We've just never been apart that long. And Ella doesn't do well with change."

Brooke takes a moment before she speaks, swishing her mouth from side to side. "It's her best friend duty to be superexcited for you. If she can't do that, you two have big-time problems."

She's right. I know she's right. But I can picture Ella's face when I tell her. Her disappointed, I'm-going-to-miss-you-so-much-I-can't-stand-it face.

"I don't know how to tell her," I say. "And I leave a week from Monday."

Brooke pulls some chips out of the cupboard. "The longer you wait, the worse it's going to be."

"I know."

"You want me to tell her?" she asks.

I almost spit out an *Oh no, definitely not* before I realize how bad that sounds. "No, thanks. I have to do it on my own."

Not satisfied with the chips, Brooke goes to the fridge and gets some dip.

"Please don't tell Ella," I beg, because I'm not convinced my last answer is enough to make it superclear.

"I won't," says Brooke. But something in my gut makes me realize I'm not sure if I can trust her.

CHAPTER TWENTY NINE

Ella

I'M AT AN OPEN HOUSE FOR A SCHOOL I don't want to go to. Ugh. Mom is having a blast though, chatting with all her old high school friends who now have kids going to Mensing.

I finally see Kali and head over to her. Mom nods and keeps talking.

"Isn't this great?" asks Kali. She's so enthusiastic I feel bad being such a grump about the whole thing.

"Yeah, I guess so," I say.

"Come on," she says. "I'll show you some of the a-*may*-zing things about this school."

She takes me to the art room, which is beyond

incredible. Student projects line the tile walls.

"Every year they pick select seniors to do a mural. It's a total honor," says Kali.

Next we go to the music room. Not that I'm musically inclined, but this place is beautiful. The leveled floor is full of music stands, and pictures of the band and orchestra from previous years are all over the walls.

"This is great," I say, "But I'm not really an artist or a musician."

"You haven't seen the pool," says Kali.

She takes me to the almost-Olympic-size pool where spectator stands with real fold-up chairs (not uncomfortable metal bleachers) surround one half of the pool.

"Impressive," I say. "But I'm not a swimmer, either."

"Okay," she says. "You're going to make this tough on me, I see. But wait until you meet Mr. Blanchard."

The halls are now full of people checking out the place. I send a quick text to Mom letting her know I'm getting the grand tour from Kali. I'm sure she thinks I'll be more excited about it if a friend shows me around, so she's fine with it.

Kali takes me into the guidance office and sneaks me into one of the rooms. A tall guy with dark hair is talking with another parent, but as soon as he sees Kali, he wraps up the conversation.

"Kali, how are you?" he says with a whole ton of enthusiasm. He turns to me. "And who is this? A new Mensing student I hope."

"This is Ella," says Kali. "She's coming here in the fall."

I totally mean to give Kali a look, but before I get the chance, Mr. Blanchard has my hand wrapped in both of his for a firm handshake.

"Pleasure to meet you, Ella," he says. "Have a seat, girls. I suppose you'd like a sneak peek at the courses we're offering next year."

Kali smiles and turns from me to Mr. Blanchard. "Actually, I was hoping you could go over some of the extracurricular activities for El."

He nods and pulls out a red folder from his drawer. "Now, this here is top secret. Haven't shown it to anyone yet," he says, patting the folder. "But Kali's family is very dear to my heart, so I'm going to share it with you."

Kali is practically bouncing in her seat, but I'm wondering what the big deal is. I'm sure it's the same lineup they have at Jefferson High.

Mr. Blanchard slides the red folder in front of us, and Kali gives me the silent go-ahead with her eyes. I pull it open and flip through the papers inside to make sure my eyes aren't tricking me.

Lists, rules, organized everything. I think I'm in love. "It's so beautiful," I say.

"Oh, right, I know I'm a bit over the top with organization," says Mr. Blanchard. "But it helps keep me sane."

Now I see why Kali wanted me to meet this particular guidance counselor.

"Yeah, yeah, organized, schmorganized, check out the extracurriculars," says an impatient Kali.

There sure is the usual—student council, athletics, maybe National Honor Society—but there's more. So much more.

A trip to Washington in the spring for the Citizenship Club. A weekend in the Adirondacks for the Environment Club. There's even a group that helps new students deal with the change of a new school and new friends by assigning buddies to the freshmen. I could so use that.

It goes on and on with all kinds of things I'm already dying to sign up for.

But when I feel my heart start beating faster at the excitement of it all, I flip the folder closed. I'm not going to Mensing.

"Thanks, but I'm only doing this to make my mom happy," I say. "I'm going to Jefferson High in the fall."

Mr. Blanchard gives Kali a look to which she scrunches up her face and shakes her head.

"Well, I'm sorry to hear you won't be joining us, Ella," he says. "But if you do change your mind, please feel free to call me." He hands me his business card, and I tuck it away in my purse. Not that I'm going to use it.

Mr. Blanchard stands up as another parent comes in. "Thanks for stopping by, girls. Always great to see you, Kali."

He gives us both a fist bump, and when I see the colorful Starburst in a glass dish on his desk, I officially dub him the coolest guidance counselor there ever was.

We walk out of his office. Kali is ready to give me the rest of the tour, but I honestly don't think I can take any more. This place is too tempting. I remind myself that Skyler isn't here, so it's not even an option.

"I think I should find my mom," I say.

Kali looks disappointed but not surprised. "Okay, but give it a chance, all right?"

I nod, even though we both know I don't mean it. I can't mean it. I couldn't possibly go here. Right?

CHAPTER THIRTY

Skyler

10. Host a fancy dinner
(eating pizza on china and inviting siblings counts)

ELLA AND I HAVE PLANNED OUT EVERY last detail of the "fancy dinner" we're hosting. Okay, Ella planned most of it, but I put everything in motion. We decided to go with more than just ordering pizza and inviting siblings, since we eat pizza all the time and there's only Ella's little brother to invite.

Everyone is bringing a dish to pass. That's how you say it in grown-up talk, a dish to pass. Ella and her mom have made some kind of casserole, and while I had hoped my mom would help me out, she had to work, and it was Dad to the rescue. And well, he's actually the better cook, anyway. We made some fancy-schmancy appetizers with crescent rolls and cream cheese with a bunch of veggies on top.

When the others get to Ella's house, they're all carrying some kind of dish. Except for Travis, who has a huge tub of water balloons for later. We gave him an out on the food. Ella and I take the dishes from Kali, Quinn, and Brooke and set them on the counter. I cannot wait to tear into the pretty desserts that Brooke and Quinn brought.

Since we're going for fancy, we also decided to dress up. The girls are in summer dresses, and Travis is in nice pants and a dress shirt he wore to his cousin's wedding. Even I have to admit he's pretty darn cute. I mean, he even combed his hair. Brooke is quick to tell him so and is already glued to his side, which Travis doesn't seem to mind. Quinn is helping Kali set the table while Ella and I heat up a couple of the dishes that need to be warm.

"We're not really doing the china plates, are we?" I ask. It was the plan, so I shouldn't be surprised that's what Ella is sticking to.

"Of course we are," says Ella. "My parents okayed it. We just have to be really careful."

We all turn and say, "Travis."

He smiles. "I know, I know. I will be a total gentleman

and won't break anything. I'm not as cray cray as you all think I am."

I laugh, because I'm actually kinda happy the "cray cray" is back. And I surprise myself by how much Travis is starting to grow on me.

We even get out the fancy wine glasses and fill them with water. It takes a little practice to fit my face in the right position to drink out of one, but eventually I get the hang of it. Travis does not. Water ends up all over his nicely ironed shirt.

We start with the appetizers, and mine is a big hit. Quinn's taco dip is also superdelicious. (She went all out and brought two dishes to pass.)

Around the table are five of my friends. A much bigger circle than Ella and I started with this summer. It makes my insides relax and my heart beat a little faster to know Ella is on board with growing up a little. With being excited to make new friends and try new things.

When the dinner dishes come out, I'm amazed at Ella's green bean casserole. I didn't even know I liked green beans. And my first bite of Kali's potato curry is both a shock to my system with all the spices and a party in my belly at the same time.

"This is so good, Kali," I say. And the others echo my words.

"Thanks," she says. "My mom is such a great cook, and this has inspired me to learn a few things from her."

"See," says Ella, "it's already turning out to be one of the best things on the list."

It is. Until dessert comes out.

Quinn's monkey bread is seriously addicting.

"It's easy," says Quinn. "You take biscuit dough and dip it in butter, then roll it around in a sugar and cinnamon mixture. Then you stick it all together in a Bundt pan and bake it."

We all pull at the little dough balls until half the thing is gone.

"Save room for mine," says Brooke. "Pineapple upside-down cake."

We each take a piece, and my mouth waters just looking at it. Fancy dinners sure do make you full, but there's always room for more dessert. Everyone takes a bite and oohs and aahs at how delicious it is.

Except Ella.

She spits out the bite in her mouth before she even chews it and puts her hand over her lips. "What did you say this was?" she asks in a muffled voice.

"Pineapple upside-down cake," says Brooke. "Why?"

"What else is in it?" asks Ella.

And although I can't see her lips, I realize what must be happening.

Ella puts her hands to her cheeks, which are now turning red.

"Is there lime in here?" I ask.

"I don't know," says Brooke. "My mom made it."

We all turn and give her a look, not just for breaking the rules, but for being so nonchalant about what's happening.

"Find out!" I shout. I rush to the drawer to get Ella's Benadryl as Brooke gets on the phone with her mom. "Here, take this," I say to Ella.

She chews the medicine as Kali and Quinn rush to get her a cold cloth.

"Is she okay?" asks Travis.

"Yeah, but she's allergic to lime," I say, guiding Ella to the couch as Quinn and Kali give her the cloth. "She's fine if she gets the Benadryl quickly."

Brooke hangs up the phone and comes over to us. "I guess you don't need me to confirm that there's lime in there," she says. "Sorry. Apparently it's my mom's secret ingredient."

I wish her apology was a little more genuine, but it isn't. Okay, sure, Ella should have told everyone she's allergic to lime if she's having a dinner party, but shouldn't a person feel a little bit bad about what's happening?

"I'll be fine," says Ella through huge, puffed lips and a bright-red face. "You didn't know."

If I'd just heard the words, I would have thought everything was fine between them. But I also see their faces, and it's clear neither one of them is happy.

"I didn't know," Brooke insists.

"That's what I said," says Ella. "You didn't know."

"I didn't," says Brooke with an even firmer tone.

Travis looks back and forth. "Is it just me, or are they having the same conversation over and over?"

"Should we go get her parents?" ask Kali.

"Is that really necessary?" asks Brooke. "Her face is getting better and her lips, well . . ."

"Yeah, we should let them know," I say. "But she'll be fine. This has happened before."

Kali runs off to get Mr. and Mrs. Wade, who are quick to come in to check on her. My nerves calm down a bit when they take it all in stride.

"She took her medicine?" asks Mrs. Wade.

"Yes, I got it to her right away," I say.

"She's lucky to have you, Skyler." Mr. Wade pats me on the back and smiles, then turns to Ella. "You feeling okay, honey?"

"Yes. Just a little embarrassed is all," says Ella.

"Oh, sweetie, don't you worry about that," says Mrs. Wade. "We all just want you to feel better."

Everyone nods and says some form of yes, yeah, yup, or uh-huh.

"Call us if you need us," says Mr. Wade. "Looks like your friends have it under control." And her parents head upstairs to let us finish our party. Although I know from experience, it's going to be a while before she feels better.

"Should we go do the water balloons?" asks Brooke.

"How about a movie?" suggests Quinn. "I think Ella could use a little break."

"Yeah, okay," says Brooke. Then she meanders over to the table to finish her dessert.

CHAPTER THIRTY-ONE

Skyler

11. Have a water balloon fight

WE WATCH AN ENTIRE MOVIE, AND ELLA'S face is getting back to normal. I don't dare mention that we still need to take a picture.

Brooke is back in the kitchen as soon as it ends, and I go to check on her.

"You okay?" I ask.

"I'm sorry I've been acting like this, Skyler," she apologizes. "I seriously don't know why I'm so jealous of you and Ella."

I had a feeling that's what's been going on.

"Quinn's your best friend," I say. "And you have,

187

like, a million friends. Why would you be jealous of me and Ella?"

Brooke sits down on one of the chairs around the kitchen table. "Quinn's not into a lot of the stuff I am. She doesn't care about getting to wear makeup, or dressing up, or even boys. But you do."

"Ella doesn't care about that stuff either," I say. "Except *maybe* boys."

"See, that's what I'm saying," says Brooke. "Don't you think you and I are a better fit?"

I'm kind of surprised by the question. "We don't trade friends because we like different things, Brooke. I still like plenty of the same things Ella does."

"I'm just saying we should be able to do those things and not be held back because they don't want to," she says. "Like your trip to Europe."

I put my finger over my lips to shush her. I'm suddenly very aware that both Ella and Quinn are in the next room.

"Don't worry. I won't say anything," she says. "But you do have to tell her."

"I will."

Travis comes into the kitchen and sends a big goofy smile at Brooke. "Ella says she's ready for the water balloon fight. I just have to change."

Brooke and I stand up.

"Do not tell Ella," I whisper. She pushes her lips together and pretends to zip them shut.

We head outside with the others and wait while Travis changes into more appropriate water-balloon-fight gear. The girls' summer dresses will hold up just fine.

Once he's ready, Travis is raring to go. "All righty now, I have one hundred balloons in this here bin," he says. "That's approximately, um, let's see, there are six of us, so . . ."

"About sixteen," says Ella. "But let's just have at it."

Her face is so much better with barely a hint of red anymore. But her lips are a different story.

"Should we do teams?" I ask, immediately regretting it. I have a flashback to letterboxing. "Or, you know, not."

I figure Brooke will jump in and claim me, but it's Ella who speaks first.

"I'll take Kali and Quinn," she says directly to Brooke. "You want Skyler and Travis, right?"

Oh man, I'd hoped the tension between them would at least be a bit less after the dinner. If only there had been no lime in that cake.

"Sounds good to me," says Brooke. And everyone

grabs as many water balloons as they can fit into their arms. Travis is seriously stocked up.

"What are the rules?" I ask.

"There's just one," says Ella.

We all wait. Ella's never had just one.

"The only rule is that there are no rules," she says. And without any warning, she shouts, "Go!"

Everyone launches what they have in their arsenal. Ella is the first to get hit, by Brooke. Then Quinn, Travis, Kali, and me. After a couple minutes, not one of us is dry. Most of us are laughing, except Ella and Brooke who continue to launch the water balloons with a fire in their eyes.

"What is your problem, Ella?" shouts Brooke, sending another water balloon at Ella's shoulder.

"*My* problem?" asks Ella. "You're the one who's been trying to take Skyler every chance you get."

Seriously, what is up with this?

I put a hand out. "Whoa. You two need to cool it."

But they don't listen. More water balloons fly through the air, and the rest of the group has now stopped to watch.

"Skyler *wants* to hang out with me. She *wants* to do new things," says Brooke. "That's not my fault."

"Yeah? That's fine. But you don't have to be such

a snob about it." Ella flings a big red water balloon at Brooke.

"Travis, do something," I say. "Please."

"Come on, ladies." Travis makes the mistake of stepping in between them. He ducks when two more water balloons go flying through the air. When he stands back up, he brings out his serious voice. "Stop it! Enough with all this girl drama. Skyler is leaving for Europe next week, and you're wasting your time fighting?"

There's a sudden chill in the air, and I swear the world has stopped turning.

Travis slaps a hand over his mouth.

Brooke punches him in the shoulder.

Everyone else turns to me with wide eyes. Especially Ella.

CHAPTER THIRTY-TWO

Ella

I CANNOT POSSIBLY HAVE HEARD THE words "Skyler is leaving for Europe next week." But I swear I just totally did. No one is saying anything, and I'm too shocked to even control what comes out of my mouth.

"You're *what*?" I ask Skyler.

She looks like a mix of caught and terrified, which I guess go pretty well together.

"I was going to tell you, Ella," she mutters.

"How long will you be gone?" I ask. But I have too many questions, so I spit them out all at once. "Who are you going with? And where are you going? I mean, when will you be home? Is this like a little trip or a big, big trip?"

"A month. My mom. Italy. And I'll be home just before school starts," she answers. "Unless she gets the account. Then I'll be there for a year."

My mouth drops open. "A *year*? That's bigger-than-any-news-ever *huge*. Why didn't you tell me?"

Travis tries again to jump in, but Skyler turns to him with laser eyes. "Travis, I will deal with you and Brooke later."

I can't believe my ears again. "*Brooke* knew?" I ask. "Why would you tell Brooke and Travis and not your best friend?"

My heart is pounding, and I reach in my pocket for a Starburst, but they're a wet mess like I am at this point. My lips start to burn again with all the blood rushing to my face.

"She overheard me talking to my mom," says Skyler, turning to Brooke with a stare you wouldn't wish upon your worst enemy. "And Brooke must have told Travis."

Travis takes a cautious step backward. "Yeah, well maybe Travis is keeping a few too many secrets these days," he says.

"What's that supposed to mean?" asks Skyler.

Uh-oh. I'm in trouble if I don't stop him.

"Why don't you guys go inside so Skyler and I can

talk?" I say. But I underestimate Travis's loyalty to Brooke.

"Not if Brooke is gonna be the one in trouble," he says. "It's you two who are hiding things from each other."

Everyone stays silent, except for Kali, who leans over and whispers, "You need to tell her, El. Like, right now."

"Will someone please tell me what's going on?" asks Skyler.

But I can't. She'll flip. So instead I try to divert attention.

"Yeah, my best friend is taking off to Italy and didn't tell me about it," I say. I grab a towel and wipe off my face, trying to buy time. But no Plan B comes to me.

"But what is Travis talking about?" asks Brooke. "What secrets?"

Only Kali, Travis, and I know what all his cryptic words mean. Kali won't talk, but I'm pretty sure Travis is about to explode.

Yup.

"Ella isn't volunteering out of the goodness of her heart," he blurts out. And while I expect him to take the easy way out and hide behind Brooke, he stands tall and stares back at me. "I'm sorry, Ella, but I can't take all this emotional girl stuff anymore. Let's just get it over with."

Skyler shakes her head and a few water droplets hit me in the face from her sopping wet hair.

"What?" asks Skyler. "Just tell us already."

"Ask Ella about Mensing," says Travis. "Go ahead, ask."

Skyler focuses only on me, and I have no idea how to get out of this. Don't I get to be mad at *her* for a bit before I confess?

"What about Mensing?" she asks me directly.

"It's not a big deal," I say, trying to play it off. "My mom thinks it would be good for me. You know my mom, once she gets an idea in her head."

"So you're going?" asks Skyler.

"No, I mean, I told my mom I wasn't, but . . ." I do a one-eighty so I don't have to face her.

"But what?" asks Skyler.

"But I think I've decided . . ." I can't seem to spit it out no matter how hard I try.

"You've decided to go," Skyler finishes for me.

All I can do is nod.

"And you didn't tell me," she says.

Her words hurt. They sting me. I whip myself back to face her. Everyone is still watching, like they can't turn away from the train wreck going on right in front of them.

"No, I didn't tell you," I say with way too much attitude. "Because I thought you'd be mad. You're so excited about high school, and I haven't been, but now

I am. I actually am." I stop and take a deep breath. "It's just that I'm excited about a different high school."

When the words run through my ears, I hear them for the first time—I really am excited about high school.

"You thought I'd be *mad?*" Skyler's voice goes higher as she stresses that last word. "Didn't you think I might be even angrier that you *didn't* tell me?"

I stand still, soaking wet, trying desperately to stay strong. I bite my lip and squeeze my fists until my fingernails send sharp pains through the palms of my hands. But when I finally speak, my voice comes out soft and weak. "I never thought I'd want to go there, Skyler. You have to believe me," I say. "And I didn't want to upset you over something that wasn't going to happen." I turn to the others and then focus on Travis. "Thanks a lot, Travis."

He's the easygoing lone guy in this wacky group, but as his eyebrows arch into a V and his shoulders hunch into Hulk pose, I wish I could take it back. "Someday, someone is going to have to explain girls to me," he says with a fierce tone in his voice. "This is ridiculous. There's no point in hiding anything from each other. Don't you two get that?"

No one says a word as we wait to see if there's more to come.

Brooke silently takes Travis by the hand and nods to Quinn and Kali to follow. The four of them sit on the deck chairs—far enough away to give us privacy, but close enough to break up a possible screaming match.

What I want more than anything is to turn back the clock and stop all of this from happening. But I can't. Skyler's eyes are sad, and I imagine mine look just as miserable.

"Why didn't you tell me about Europe?" I ask almost in a whisper.

"I didn't want to upset you." Skyler kicks at the grass, and now she won't even look at me.

It's quiet, except for the *chit, chit, chit* of the sprinkler next door.

Why can't it just be like it used to be?

I want to say something, anything, but my lungs are refusing to give me the air I need to do it.

I was so sure the list would help us. Now everything is a big I-can't-fix-this mess.

My heart beats tiny little beats like it's much too tired to do any more work right now. I wonder if she feels the same way.

Skyler crouches down, grabs the last water balloon, and squeezes it until it bursts.

"You know what, Ella? Maybe I didn't want you

raining on my parade either. Maybe that's why I didn't tell you." She stands up and looks me right in the eye. "Because I'm so happy about this, and I didn't want you to—"

"To ruin it?" I ask, cutting her off. The anger comes rushing back through every part of me. This isn't all my fault.

"Yeah," says Skyler, standing her ground. "Like you're doing right now."

I close my eyes and swallow hard. And that's really it. What else is there to say? Skyler has been my best friend for as long as I can remember, but there's no going back from this.

"Well I'm sorry I ruined everything," I say. "I'll just go." I grab the towel and head for the front yard.

Kali comes running after me. "Are you okay?" she asks.

I don't answer.

"Ella, where are you going?" she tries again. "This is *your* house."

I stop and turn to her, tears now streaming down my face.

"I just need to be alone right now." I pick up the pace and head down the driveway.

Funny thing is, I don't think I'll need to ask to be alone after today.

CHAPTER THIRTY-THREE

Skyler

IT'S BEEN FOUR DAYS SINCE THE BIG fight with Ella. Four days. That's officially the longest we've ever gone without talking to each other. Which makes it weird that I don't miss her terribly like I expected.

I mean sure, I'm still a little mad. I wonder how she could keep something like going to a different high school from me. And then my brain reminds me that I lied to her too.

But these last four days have been fun, not miserable. Brooke, Quinn, and I went to a concert at Towne Park with a big group of friends. It's a local band that's starting to hit the big time. Brooke and I had a spa day, with full-out pedicures and manicures. My mom took me shopping for the trip, and I got a cute new pair of sneakers for all the walking we plan on doing.

And with every day that goes by, I'm less and less mad, and more and more accepting of the fact that Ella and I are just going in different directions. Literally.

But I'm pretty sure she's been home sulking for four days, waiting for me to call her. Not gonna happen.

Mom has insisted I clean my room before we leave so I'll have a nice clean place to come back to, or something like that. But, she is taking me to Italy, so I grant her her wish.

It's not until I start cleaning my desk that I come across my copy of the BFF Summer Bucket List with everything but the last three checked off. I grab a pen and sit down, putting big check marks next to "Host a fancy dinner" and "Water balloon fight."

After the dinner party, I'd made the group get together for pictures in all their wet clothes, holding the "dish to pass" they each brought. Of course I didn't tell Ella this since she walked out in a huff.

One more to go.

And I swear the last item on the list stares at me.

12. Speak actual words to our crushes.

The one I insisted we add. The only one standing in the way of completing this list.

Do I care if we don't finish the list?

I stare back at it, but it keeps taunting me. Eleven things accomplished. One to go.

I read through each one, remembering both the fun moments and the not-so-great ones.

THE BFF SUMMER BUCKET LIST

1. Sleep outside

I seriously got Ella to watch a movie with "ghost" in the title.

2. Best friend photo shoot

I run my hand over my leg and the mark from the playground gash.

3. Face a fear

I laugh as I think of that cow. And that moo. Oh my god that moo. I grab my leg again, where the stitches have finally dissolved.

4. Get a tattoo (temporary—do I even need
to clarify that?)

The dragon tattoo is gone, but do I still have that fire inside me? I smile as I picture Penny Boy at the town fair.

5. Canoe across Towne Lake (the long
way—no cheating!)

I have to laugh again as I remember a shocked Brooke running out of the water, leaving me and Ella with the tipped over boat.

6. Go shopping in pj's and have a shopping
cart race

Oh that poor display. I will never look at a pop can the same way again.

7. Break a world record (adjustment—try to
break a world record)

Yes, there's a check mark here thanks to the unanimous decision. Ella finally gave in.

8. Random acts of kindness

This might be my favorite.

9. Go letterboxing (also, google "letterboxing"
to figure out what it actually is)

Now that I know what it actually is, I think I might try it out when Quinn and Kali go on their regular letterboxing searches. That is if Kali is still speaking to me.

10. Host a fancy dinner (eating pizza on
china and inviting siblings counts)

Dinner, great. Dessert, not so much.

11. Have a water balloon fight

Yeah. Not my finest moment.

12. Speak actual words to our crushes

Can I really let this list go unfinished?

• • •

I text Brooke and Quinn.

Need to find Penny Boy. Can you help?

I get replies back from both of them, but they pretty much say the same thing. No known get-togethers going on today.

I don't want to do it, but I also don't have much of a choice. I have no name for this kid and not one clue how to find him.

I send Travis a message.

Hope you're not mad. Can I ask a favor?

He replies quickly.

Nope. Not mad.

I start to type the message, but get startled when there's a *plink, plink* on my bedroom window. I open it up, and there's Travis down below.

"Seems kind of silly to text when I'm right next door, don't you think?" he asks. "Come down."

"I'll be right there," I say. I've avoided him this week, not sure if he's on Team Skyler or Team Ella.

Who am I kidding? I've avoided him since kinder-garten.

I make my way downstairs and find Travis sitting on our front steps. I take the spot next to him.

"I'm sorry, Travis," I say.

"For what?"

I still can't tell if the kid is clueless or the most easy-going person I've ever met.

"For being a jerk to you all these years. For getting mad that you told about Europe. For the fight," I say. "All of it."

Travis smiles. "No worries," is his simple answer.

"Really?" I ask. "Just like that? You're not upset with me?"

"That's cray cray," says Travis. "You're my friend, right?"

Oh how I wish I could let it go like he can. My heart clenches a bit when I ask my next question. "Have you seen Ella?"

Travis nods. "Yeah, we've been volunteering. And I guess she and Kali have been planning out all their activities for the fall."

I push my lips together at the thought of her going to a different high school. Although I might be at a high school even farther away anyway.

"You two will be okay you know," says Travis.

"What do you mean?" I ask.

"You and Ella. It's okay to grow apart," he says. "It's part of growing up. But it doesn't mean you can't still be friends."

I sit back to get a good look at him. "Travis, when did you get so wise?"

He chuckles. "Oh, it's not me. I told my mom the whole story, and that's what she said. Makes me sound mature and all, doesn't it?"

"It does," I say.

"Hey, what was that favor you wanted to ask me?" he says. "My new soccer friend is coming over in a few minutes, but if you need something . . ."

"Oh, it's nothing," I say. "I just wanted to finish the list is all."

Travis smiles as a shiny red car pulls into his driveway. "Well, if you need me, we'll be in the backyard." He wraps an arm around my shoulders and squeezes.

And when the car door opens, Penny Boy steps out.

CHAPTER THIRTY FOUR

Ella

I'VE NEVER GONE FOUR WHOLE DAYS without Skyler. It kind of hits me though that at least the first two weren't as hard as I thought they'd be. I've been volunteering like crazy, am way past the required hours for Mensing, and Kali and I have been planning out what we're going to sign up for in the fall. I have several lists started already. So instead of sulking like I thought I would, I've actually been keeping busy. And enjoying it.

I'm still not on board with scary movies, but Quinn did talk me into seeing a pretty goofy one I wouldn't normally even consider. And you know what? It was fun.

Skyler's been off doing all the things she wants to

do before she leaves for Europe. I know because her Instantpic photos are out of control these days. But I guess the things she wants to do don't include saying good-bye to me.

I'm not mad anymore. Not really. I mean I lied to her like she lied to me. I'm just sad that we couldn't share our biggest news with each other. We've always shared everything.

And I can't blame Brooke. I did blame her. Oh I sure as heck did. And I still say there was no need for her to act all jealous and what not. But it's not her fault Skyler and I are drifting apart. It's nobody's fault really.

But I totally was mad the first day. I had the BFF Summer Bucket List in my hands and crumpled the thing into a tiny little ball. I was ready to toss it in the trash. I really was. But something stopped me.

It wasn't finished.

And I know the rules state that we need to do each item together. We don't even have photo proof of the fancy dinner and the water balloon fight. But I decided right there that I'm not going to be the one who doesn't complete it.

So every day since, I've ridden my bike past Alex's house, hoping he'll be outside. Unfortunately, there have been no Alex sightings. Not a single one.

Today I'm going to put on my big girl shoes and be the kind of brave I usually can only be around Skyler. I'm going to his house, and I'm knocking on the door. Go ahead world, and try to stop me.

I don't usually do dresses or skirts, so my wardrobe is pretty limited in that department, but I figure a special occasion deserves a little bit of dressing up. I manage to find a cute skirt with some pink trim and a matching shirt. I throw a flowery headband in my hair and make sure my hair looks presentable. I glance at the makeup Skyler left here one of the days she tried to get me to put some on, and I consider it for a minute, but I'm afraid I might end up looking like a clown if I do it myself.

When I pass the mirror, I look more like Skyler than myself.

I change back into the shorts and blue top I had on earlier and trade the headband for a simple hair clip.

It's a three-minute walk down the street and when I get to Alex's house, there's no sign of him. But there is a car in the driveway, and when I see the little pink flip-flop air freshener, I figure it must be his mom's car.

I stand on the front lawn for way too long. A couple neighbors walk by and say hello, but they give me odd looks as I continue to stand like a statue in the middle of the yard. I have to do this.

I take one step.

And then another.

Until I'm finally at the base of the front steps.

Three more steps, Ella. You can do this.

I picture the list, the eleven completed items, and the one just sitting there laughing at me.

12. Speak actual words to our crushes.

I hop up the three steps with determination and stand in front of the door. Somehow ringing the doorbell is the piece I can't seem to make happen.

I raise my hand to it, but pull my arm back down. I turn around, ready to take off, but force myself to go back.

Just press the button. Say hello. Mission accomplished. List complete.

Yes, that's all I have to do. Say hi. And go. I can do this.

I press the doorbell and a musical chime echoes through the house. The door opens. And Alex's mom stands in front of me. "Hi. Can I help you?" she asks.

"Hi. I'm, um, I'm Ella, and I live down the street, so I was just stopping by to say hello and welcome you to the neighborhood, you know, I mean you've been here for a few weeks now, but I had some time, so here I am."

Run-on sentence, anyone? I push my lips together to get myself to stop talking.

"That's very nice of you, Ella," says Mrs. Alex's Mom. What is their last name anyway? "I have a son your age, but he's not home right now. Maybe I can send him down to say hello when he gets back?"

This was not part of the plan. Press the button. Say hello. Mission accomplished. Not Alex comes to say hello, and I have to have an actual convo with him. But it appears to be my only option.

"Yeah, sure," I say. "That would be great."

I give her my address and cell phone number.

"Where do you go to school, Ella?" she asks.

"Oh, um, I went to Washington, but I'm going to Mensing in the fall," I say.

She smiles. "Perfect. That's where Alex will be going."

I smile back and give some random reason why I have to get going: My mom is waiting for me, and I can't be late.

Mrs. Alex's Mom doesn't seem to mind my rambling at all. She simply thanks me again and lets me go on my way.

I take a deep breath. That wasn't so bad. Except for the fact that I haven't even talked to Alex yet.

And later today, he'll be coming to my house.

CHAPTER THIRTY-FIVE

Skyler

12. Speak actual words to our crushes

THE INSTANT I SEE PENNY BOY, I KNOW I'm right about him. That smile. Those eyes. What would Ella say? OH MY PENNIES.

But I can't do it. I give Travis one of my usual excuses and run into the house. I hide in my bedroom for more than thirty minutes, planted near the window with a perfect view of them throwing a baseball back and forth in Travis's backyard.

The list sits on my desk.

One. More. Challenge.

I wonder if Ella is having the same struggle. My first

instinct is to text her and ask, but that's not an option. If I'm going to do this, I have to do it now. I leave for Italy tomorrow, and I might not get another shot.

I consider throwing on a cute new outfit, but I am happy enough with what I have on. I let my hair out of the ponytail holder and attempt to do a finger comb through. I march myself past the packed suitcase on my floor. Down the stairs. Out the back door. And over to the tall wooden fence that separates our yards.

I have never been afraid to talk to a boy before. Why start now?

I step up onto the two-by-four that runs a couple feet up from the ground and boost myself up until my hands grip the top of the fence. There they are.

"Hi, Travis," I say, and I'm suddenly aware I am only a head right now to Penny Boy. My outfit doesn't even matter. I should have at least paid more attention to my hair.

"Hi." Travis looks a little surprised, but he goes into gentleman mode anyway. "Hey, Cooper, this is my friend, and next door neighbor obviously, Skyler."

"Hi," says Cooper.

Holy cow. This is it. I need one word, and I complete my part of the list. That's it. Just one.

"Didn't I see you at The Donut the day of the fire?" asks Cooper.

Answer him. Spit it out, Skyler. You will never ever forgive yourself if you don't.

But when I open my mouth to speak, my foot slips off its perch, and I spring backward to the ground. Hard.

I must have let out a screech—it's all a little blurry right now though—because in a matter of seconds, Travis and Cooper are hanging over the top of the fence.

"Are you okay?" asks Travis.

"Yeah, I'm fine," I say.

"You sure?" asks Cooper.

"Yup. My butt hurts a little, that's all," I say without even thinking.

And just like that, I've said my first words to my crush. And those first words included the word "butt." I'm not sure I could possibly be more embarrassed.

"Oh, um, your nose is bleeding," says Cooper.

I whip my fingers to my face and touch the base of my nose. Deep red blood transfers onto my fingers. I must have smacked it on the way down.

I laugh, because what else can I do at this point?

Travis has taken off, but he quickly returns with a

cloth, which he catapults through the air like the base-ball he'd been throwing.

I brace myself as I stand up and wipe at my nose with the cloth.

"I know this will sound strange," I say directing it at Cooper, "but would you mind taking a picture with me? It's kind of a summer project thing."

Travis's eyes pop a little. "Is this? You mean number twelve?"

"Mmm-hmm," I answer.

"Dude, she needs this picture," he says to Cooper.

I expect strange looks from Penny Boy, but instead he takes it all in stride and shrugs. "No problem."

He and Travis hop down and come through the gate to my backyard.

Cooper stands next to me as Travis takes out his phone. "Everyone, say 'penny.'"

Travis and I chuckle, but Cooper doesn't question it. He leans his head in next to mine and says what he's asked to.

"Send it to me?" I ask Travis.

"Yeah, okay," he says.

Cooper watches us with a curious look in his eyes. "Someday you'll explain this to me, right?"

I'm not sure that would be such a good idea. "Just

know it's for a good cause." I excuse myself to go get cleaned up as Travis and Cooper take seats on my back deck.

When the ping goes off letting me know Travis has sent the picture, I pick my phone up off the counter. And without thinking twice, I type in Ella's number.

CHAPTER THIRTY-SIX

Ella

12. Speak actual words to our crushes

MY PHONE KEEPS BEEPING WITH NEW texts, but I don't even bother to look. I am way too nervous about finishing this list and the really cute boy who is supposed to be stopping by my house any moment now.

I had considered calling Kali or even Quinn to vent, but instead I decide to curl up in front of the TV and watch one of my favorite movies. One I always used to watch with Skyler. I expect it not to be as funny without her, but I laugh as usual at all the punch lines and crazy situations the characters find themselves in.

And since I have the whole afternoon to myself, I put in another one.

The movie is right at the good part near the end when there's a knock on the door. I jump, sending my bowl of popcorn flying. I pick at the pieces on the floor, dumping them back into the bowl a handful at a time. Like if I ignore the knocking, whoever it is will go away. But I know who it is. And I don't want him to go away.

This time it's the doorbell, and I jump again. I reach for my Starburst, pop one into my mouth, and put the last one in my pocket.

I force myself to take one step toward the door. I take a deep breath and make it the rest of the way. I brush some popcorn off my clothes, scrunch my curls, and smack my cheeks a little. I'm ready.

I pull the door open with a confidence I'm not convinced I can keep up.

There's no one there.

I pull at the screen door and stick my head out.

"Oh, hi. I thought you weren't home." It's Alex. And he's standing in my driveway. "Are you Ella?" he asks, coming closer to the door.

"Mmm-hmm," I mumble, swirling what's left of the candy around in my mouth. Does that count as actual words?

"My mom said you came to my house to say hello," he says. "She sent me down here."

Say something, Ella. But no words come out.

"I can go if this is a bad time," he says, taking a step back.

Great. Now I look a wee bit crazy. And my nerves are firing a mile a minute. I reach in my pocket, but when I stare at the candy in my hand, I so badly want to be done. With depending on fruit chews to calm my nerves. With needing Skyler next to me, cheering me on to be brave. With being afraid of change.

"Wait," I shout. He stands still, like I've scared him. I put up a hold-on-a-second finger and chew at top speed so I can talk. "I'm Ella." I move down the steps closer to him, take a quiet, deep breath, and reach out a hand.

"I'm Alex."

My anxiety melts away as he shakes my hand. I even manage a smile.

"Welcome to the neighborhood, Alex," I say. "I hear you're going to Mensing."

He points to the front step as if he needs my okay, and we both sit down.

"Yeah, they have a great sports program on top of the academics, so my parents thought it was the best choice," he says. "Where do you go?"

"I'll be at Mensing in the fall too," I answer. "Have you done your volunteer hours yet?"

He leans forward with his arms on his knees. "Almost finished. I've been helping with the youth soccer program."

"That's great," I say. "I volunteer at the animal shelter."

"Oh, my friend is doing that too," he says.

"You know Kali?" I ask. Because everyone seems to know Kali.

"No, a kid from—"

But he stops when my phone goes off again.

"Do you need to get that?" he asks.

"I probably should," I say. "It hasn't stopped beeping for the last hour. I'll be right back."

I grab my phone off the counter and head back outside, checking the message on the way.

"It's my dad," I say, sitting down. There are a bunch more messages, but as soon as I text Dad back, I put the phone down next to me. I'll check later.

Alex is here.

And I'm talking to him.

"I finished the list," I say out loud.

"What?" he asks.

"Oh sorry, I just realized I finished this BFF bucket list that my friend, well, possibly ex-friend and I have been doing all summer. Would you, um, would you mind if I took a picture? We can do a selfie."

"Sure," he says, but his face twists and turns like he's confused. I guess I would be too.

We take the picture and I quickly add in Skyler's number with a little note that says "This is Alex" before I can change my mind.

SEND.

"Can I ask you something?" says Alex.

"Yeah, sure."

"I was at my friend's house earlier, you know, the one I told you about, and this girl asked me the same thing," he says.

I rack my brain to remember what question I asked him. "What do you mean?"

"She asked if I would take a picture with her," he says. "Said it was some kind of summer project. Do you know her?"

His words are swirling through my head, not making much sense, until the tornado slows down, and everything falls into place.

"Wait, are you . . . I mean . . . hold on a sec." I check my messages to see there's one from Skyler. There is.

It's a picture message.

Of Penny Boy.

I check my messages to see if there's one from Skyler. There is.

It's a picture message.

Of Penny Boy.

Penny Boy is sitting on my back deck with Travis RIGHT NOW. His name is Cooper! her text says. The time stamp is from a few hours ago.

I stare at the picture. Up at Alex. Back at the picture.

Totally the same kid.

Or . . . maybe not.

"Weird question, but is there any chance you have a twin brother?" I ask.

He eyes me like I have two heads. "Um, no. Just an older sister."

Hmm.

"Your name is Alex, right?" I ask.

"Yes, my name is Alex." He laughs and turns his shoulders toward me. "You're a little strange, you know that?"

"Yup, been told that before," I say. "Makes me unique. Is your friend's name Travis by any chance?"

"Yeah," he says, perking up. "You know him?"

I nod, still trying to process everything. "Why would he call you Cooper?"

"It is," he says. "My *first* name. Cooper is my last name. The soccer team calls me that. It's a guy thing."

I'm mesmerized by his eyes. "Oh my god, you're Penny Boy," I say quietly.

And before he can ask what on earth I'm talking about, I get a message back from Skyler.

> SERIOUSLY?! You must be joking. That is 100% Penny Boy. His name is Cooper.

I answer back.

> TOTALLY SERIOUS. Penny Boy's LAST name is Cooper. Was there a pink flip-flop air freshener in his mom's car?

She gets back to me quickly as poor Alex picks dirt off his sneaker.

> Yes! OMG. ROTFL right now!!

"I'm sorry," I say to Alex. "I have to send one more message, and then I'll explain, okay?"

"I will never understand girls," he says with a chuckle. "Go ahead."

I smile as I write back four words to Skyler.

Oh. My. ALEX. COOPER.

CHAPTER THIRTY-SEVEN

Skyler

I SERIOUSLY CANNOT BELIEVE IT WHEN I see Ella's text. Penny Boy Cooper is Ella's Alex? No way.

Although I guess it's fitting to end the summer bucket list challenge like this, since the rest of it was crazy too.

Ella sends a message that she'll text me later and also that she has no choice but to tell Alex Cooper the truth. How completely embarrassing. I'm surprised Ella has the guts to do it.

And how will she explain it anyway? "So, my best friend and I both have major crushes on you (salute and say, "Major Crushes"), but we didn't know you were you, or the same you anyway. One of us thought you were Alex, which of course you are, and the other nicknamed you Penny Boy because she pretty much stole the penny you dropped at The Donut one day and then put it in a scrapbook in case you two get married someday."

I hope she puts it better than that.

"Skyler?" Mom calls up the stairs. "Do you need anything else before we leave?"

My suitcase is packed, my backpack is full, and all my chargers and electronics are in a plastic bag. I have snacks, magazines, my favorite hairbrush, and an extra travel tube of toothpaste. I even have a list of all the things I wanted to get ready for the trip, with another list of rules for staying on track while I packed. I guess Ella has rubbed off on me.

"No, I'm all set," I yell back down.

It's quiet for a minute until the doorbell rings. A little piece of me hopes it's Ella.

But I can't remember the last time Ella actually rang my doorbell.

Mom is chatting, but the sounds are muffled. I tip-toe down the stairs to see what's up.

"Skyler, come down here," says Mom. "You have a visitor."

I race down the rest of the steps, but it's not Ella at the door.

"Oh, hey, Eduardo," I say. Mom's top photographer also makes house calls apparently.

"I finally got those pictures done for you and Ella," he says. "I am sorry it took so long. Your mom has me working hard this summer." He gives Mom a wink and hands me a big manila envelope.

"Thank you." I hold the thick envelope in my hands, and that day runs through my mind. The BFF photo shoot.

Is Ella even my friend still?

"There is a flash drive in there with the digital pictures," says Eduardo, "but I made copies of the best ones for both of you."

I smile what must be a sad looking smile.

"Is everything not okay?" he asks.

Mom wraps an arm around me and pulls me close. "A little squabble between friends. That's all."

Eduardo crouches down so our heights are the same and taps the envelope with his pointer finger. "The girls in those pictures, they're going to be friends for a long time."

"I don't know about that," I say. "We got in a pretty big fight. And we've kind of grown apart."

Eduardo takes the envelope from me and pulls out one of the photos. It's me giving Ella a piggyback ride, both of us laughing hysterically. It instantly becomes one of my favorites ever.

He holds it up to face me. "No need to be *mejores amigas*," he says. "Best friends is not necessary, you see. *Verdaderas amigas*. Yes."

There has always been something seriously cool about the way Eduardo speaks. Like he sees something special through the lens of that camera and can explain it like no one else can.

"What does that mean?" I ask.

"True friends. Not best, just true," he translates. "Someone who has touched your life will always stay in your heart." He puts his hand over his own heart.

I take the pictures from him. "*Verdaderas amigas*," I repeat. "Thank you, Eduardo."

He holds out his fist for a bump. "You are very welcome."

"I'll be back in a bit, okay, Mom?"

Mom gives me the okay, and I take off running toward Ella's.

Alex Cooper is gone when I get to Ella's house, and she's sitting on her front steps staring out at nothing.

"Hi," I say.

She looks up and smiles. "Hi."

"Is it okay if I sit down?" I ask.

Ella pats the spot next to her. I sit and hand over the envelope.

"Eduardo just dropped these off," I say. "I thought I should get them to you before I go."

Ella opens the envelope and pulls out the photos. We check them out one by one, not saying a word, but I can tell both of us are remembering that day.

"They're great," she says. "Thanks."

"Sure. Eduardo says no matter what, the girls in those pictures are *verdaderas amigas*," I say, doing my best to get the accent right.

"True friends," says Ella. "I like that."

We're silent for a minute, and then Ella gets up like there's a fire. "I have something for you too."

When she comes back, she has her own stack of photos.

"Congratulations," she says. "We've officially completed the BFF Summer Bucket List. I collected them from everyone. Thought we should each have a copy of our adventures."

We flip through, smiling and laughing with every memory.

Sleeping outside, the photo shoot, facing our fears, getting tattoos, canoeing across Towne Lake the long way, going shopping in our pj's and having an epic (yet disastrous) shopping cart race, almost breaking a world record, doing random acts of kindness, going letter-boxing, hosting a fancy dinner, having a water balloon fight, and speaking actual words to our crushes. She must have just printed out the last one before I got here.

"I'm sorry for everything, Ella," I say.

"I'm sorry too."

I can't deny that things have changed between us, but my shoulders relax and my heart feels whole again knowing we're still friends.

"You're going to love Mensing," I say.

Ella kicks her feet out and leans back on her hands. "I hope so," she says. "And you're going to love Europe."

"It'll definitely be a new experience," I say.

Ella turns to me. "I'm really happy for you and your mom you know. This will be so good for both of you."

And when her words reach me, tears trickle down my cheeks. Because if anyone understands why this trip is so important to me, it's Ella.

She throws her arms around me, and we hug like we have nowhere else to be. Except that we do.

"I have to go," I say. "My dad wants to have dinner

together tonight since Mom and I leave tomorrow."

Ella nods.

"I'm meeting Kali and Travis at Three Scoops for ice cream later. We're celebrating finishing our volunteer hours," says Ella. "Alex might even be there. If you have some time to stop by."

I laugh. "You mean he didn't run away screaming when you told him the truth?"

"Nope," says Ella. "He actually thought it was pretty funny. So will you come?"

"I'd like that," I say.

"I'll even invite Brooke and Quinn if you want," says Ella.

"Yeah, that would be great. What time?" I ask.

"Eight o'clock," she says.

I give Ella's hand a squeeze. "I'll be there."

CHAPTER THIRTY-EIGHT

Ella

I STAND HERE IN FRONT OF THE COUNTER AT
Three Scoops, debating whether to get peanut butter
swirl or black raspberry, my two favorite flavors, as Kali,
Travis, and Alex check the board. I read every one of
the forty-seven choices, practically tasting and smelling
them all.

Brooke and Quinn come through the doors, and
all the introductions are made to Alex Cooper. Brooke
must recognize him, because she does a double take as
she shakes his hand. She turns to me and whispers, "Is
that Penny Boy?"

I nod. "Yeah, *and* Alex. One in the same."

She laughs a quiet laugh as Alex turns his attention to Travis. "No way," she says.

"Way," I answer.

The whole group of us waits without saying why. No one makes a move to order.

"I don't think she's coming," says Brooke. "You said eight o'clock. It's eight ten."

And I wonder if maybe my Skyler-radar might not be on target anymore. The clock changes to 8:11.

One more minute. Give her one more minute.

"She probably has a lot to get ready, El," says Kali, clearly trying to prepare me for the possibility that Skyler might not show up. "It's a big trip."

But Travis without his filter jumps in. "Nah, she's been ready for a week," he says.

"Maybe spending more time with her dad then," says Quinn.

I attempt a smile, but I'm pretty sure it comes out more like a sad clown.

"No, she'll be here," I say.

The hands on the clock continue to move, but we all stand perfectly still. *Ticktock. Ticktock.*

And at exactly 8:12, Skyler walks through the door. "Right on time," I say to myself.

"Sorry I'm late," she says, still oblivious to her ability to be late, yet strangely punctual.

Everyone else orders mouthwatering flavors like Triple-Chocolate Lava, Snickers Supreme, and Cotton-Candy Carnival. Skyler and I are next at the counter.

We both study the board again and then each other.

"Pistachio," we say in unison.

"Yes, pistachio in cones, please," I say.

On the way to the booth, Skyler stops me and hands me a small gift bag.

"This is for you," she says. "I made one for me too."

I move the tissue paper and pull out a sparkly pink frame with gemstones around the edge. Inside is a copy of the BFF bucket list with all the little boxes checked off. But there's a new challenge at the end.

"I hope you don't mind," says Skyler. "I added one more."

13. Have a great adventure

I smile thinking about what this means for both of us.

"I know it might not be one we do together, but I thought it should be on the list," she says.

"Agreed. But pictures are still required," I add with

a smile. I hug the frame. "It's perfect. Thank you."

And then I get a giant hug from Skyler.

We squeeze into the booth with the others, careful not to drop our ice cream as everyone scoots over.

"You two tried them all, so which one is the best?" Quinn asks.

I think for a moment about my favorites, but come up with a more accurate answer. "They're all different," I say with a glance at Skyler.

"Yeah, and you can't have too many flavors," she says. "Or too many friends."

She smiles, and while I know things won't be the same for us from now on, we'll always be friends somehow. I hold up my cone to toast. "To true friends," I say.

Everyone follows suit and holds up their sundaes, banana splits, and dishes full of ice cream. And in perfect sync, like we've all been friends forever, we clink desserts.

"To true friends."

The BFF Thank-You List

An enormous, heartfelt thank-you to all of you who have come along on this adventure:

• My wonderful agent, Uwe Stender, who encourages me, goes to bat for me, and makes me a better writer with each story. My editor, Alyson Heller, who treasures "lifer" friends as much as I do. The talented Aladdin team who made this book happen and created the perfect cover.

• My critique partners from the beginning—Jen Maschari, Summer Heacock, Triona Murphy, and Kim Chase. My first CPs, Bill McCambley and Bekezela Broscius. For reading and support—Emily Cushing, Marieke Nijkamp, Gail Nall, Brenda Drake, Kellie DuBay Gillis, Elaine Vickers, Kristin Gray, Stephanie Wass, Jessica Collins.

• For this book specifically, huge thanks go out to Dana Edwards, Janet Sumner Johnson, Jenny Lundquist, and my lobster, Jen Malone, as well as mother-daughter teams Beth, Hailey, and Claire; and Sara and Grace for their spot-on feedback.

• My writing group—Kate, Claudia, and Sandi. And Adrienne, who the term "BFF" should have been invented for. BNCWI, SCBWI, The Guild, and the Sweet Sixteens for such supportive communities.

• My Maplemere sixth-grade class, and my first crush—so much of you guys goes into everything I write. Sweet Home Middle, my East Side fourth-grade class, and my Riverview family for helping me create an amazing bank of memories to draw from.

• My wonderful friends for all your much-needed support. And my FLGT girls, you are the true meaning of friendship. If ever there was a group who proved you can grow in different directions and remain the best of friends, it is this one.

• My extended family, I appreciate you so very much.

• My dad, who instilled in me the value of education and the power of reading. My mom, who encouraged me and celebrated every success with unparalleled enthusiasm. I love you both so very much, and Mom, I miss you every single day.

• My husband for his unyielding support and belief in me. And for eating pistachio ice cream with me to celebrate.

• My incredible kids, Nathan and Kiley, who inspire me each day. You two make this all worthwhile. Thank you for being a part of this with me. I love you the whole wide world.